The Beautiful Coat

and

Other Assorted Stories for Children

by

Michael Angus

Illustrations by Katharine Sarah Angus

ISBN-13: 9781484832233
ISBN-10: 148483223X

For Katie

Contents

List of Illustrations

*All illustrations by Katharine Sarah Angus, aged 9 (except *, by Christopher Angus, aged 3).*

Acknowledgements

My thanks go especially to my daughter Katie, the inspiration for many of these stories, directly and indirectly. She helped me immeasurably, to develop storylines, by giving me titles and ideas, and for providing the illustrations: her wonderful drawings and renderings.

To Christopher also, my son: my thanks for his inspiration by his easy cheeky laugh and constant 'tocking'.

To my mother, and to Auntie Susie: 'boldly go' my thanks for the proof reading and complimentary and invaluable critique (not to mention the unbiased enthusiasm!).

To Jill Maden: my thanks, for her sound and generous advice regarding publishing (and my admiration too, for her ability to lean into life's bends!)

To Colin McNeish, for those opportunities, albeit brief and few in number but treasured none the less, to share thoughts on faith and belief, in spite of our 'differences'.

My sincere thanks also to Café 19, Helensburgh, for plentiful supply of coffee and companionable solitude, thanks and respect also to those who volunteer and support, and lastly, to the inspiration that made 'the beautiful coat': this really really could not have been written without you.

Michael Angus
October 2013

Foreword

The following fifteen stories were written, primarily, for children of all ages. There is no particular order, and no intended theme, other than at the time of writing I was thinking hard on my life, my values, the choices I'd made and the consequences thereof.

Mostly I was thinking about worth, and the things in life that impact upon our appreciation of our own worth, not least our perceptions of ourselves. As I read these stories back I cannot help but notice how much this influenced the writing, at a time when I was noticing too in my own children how early it starts, those inexplicable worries that can assault us, with immunity and without reason.

The writing of these stories was therefore driven, on the whole, by an implicit incentive: to try and dispel the consequence of such worries. Doubtless they will not have the capacity to do so as entirely as intended, but perhaps they might at least offer some comfort to my children, indeed to any child, to know that they are not alone – that there are other shadows, lying all around.

And by any child I mean, of course, of any age, any age whatsoever............

At the risk of stating the obvious, I sincerely hope that you, and your children, enjoy the reading of them.

MA
October 2013

THE PENGUIN, THE CENTIPEDE, THE RABBIT AND THE TREE

Once upon a time there were four friends: a penguin, a centipede, a rabbit and a tree. The four friends were all very close, as close in fact as friends could possibly be, and the whole school knew it. Rarely, if ever, would they be seen apart, whether in the classroom, in the playground, when they were coming to or going home from school. Even when they weren't at school, at weekends or during the holidays, they would *still* always be together. And it seemed to everyone that, regardless of where they were or what they were doing, the four friends were utterly content, and truly happy to be in each others company, forever laughing and joking, no matter what, rain or shine. Their unabashed enthusiasm for everything and anything was infectious, and it made the four friends very popular: everyone, absolutely *everyone*, loved being in their company too!

One day, the school announced that it was going to have a sports' day. Well, the four friends couldn't wait for the big day to come. They were *very* excited, and just couldn't stop talking about how excited they were and how much they were looking forward to taking part in all the various events.

The penguin was always heard saying: 'I can't wait for the running races – I'll run as fast as the wind!'

The centipede was always heard saying: 'I can't wait for the high jump – I'll jump as high as a mountain!'

And the rabbit was always heard saying: 'I can't wait for the swimming races – I'll swim faster than a speed boat!'

But the tree couldn't decide which event it was looking forward to, so it mostly just kept quiet, and if asked, would say: 'I think it will be a wonderful day, to see all my friends do so well in their favourite events.'

The big sports' day eventually arrived, and the whole school turned out, everyone as desperately keen to take part, but also to see how the four friends would get on.

First were the running races. The penguin put absolutely everything he could into it, this being *his* event after all, and he ran as fast as he possibly could. But he had such short, scrawny legs and also, because of his large flabby webbed feet, he could hardly run at all. In fact, he was just rubbish at it! He more wobbled round the course than ran round it! The centipede on the other hand, because he had lots and lots and *lots* of legs, could run incredibly fast, in fact he could run as fast as the wind! He ran so much faster than everyone else, including his friend the penguin, and everyone clapped and cheered when he won.

The penguin was very sad that he did not win, and was embarrassed that he had done so badly. The tree of course couldn't run at all, so it came last.

Next were the jumping events. The centipede put absolutely everything *he* could into it, this being *his* event after all, and he jumped as high as he possibly could. But he had such weak, skinny legs and also, because he had such a long squirmy body, he could hardly jump at all. In fact, he was just rubbish at it! He could hardly even get off the ground - he more wriggled like a mad wriggly thing than jumped! The rabbit on the other hand, because she had such big strong hind-legs, could jump incredibly high; in fact she could jump as high as a mountain! She jumped so much higher than everyone else, including her friend the centipede, and everyone clapped and cheered when she won.

The centipede was very sad that he did not win, and was embarrassed that he had done so badly. The tree of course couldn't jump at all, so it came last.

Next were the swimming races. The rabbit put absolutely everything she could into it, this being *her* event after all, and she swam as fast as she possibly could. But she had such short, puny arms and also, because she had such a fat furry body, she could hardly swim at all. In fact, she was just rubbish at it! She didn't so much swim as sink like a big, soggy stone! The penguin on the other hand, because he had such a smooth sleek body and massive webbed feet, could swim incredibly fast; in fact he could swim as fast as a speed boat! He swam so much faster than everyone else, including his friend the rabbit, and everyone clapped and cheered when he won.

The rabbit was very sad that she did not win, and was embarrassed that she had done so badly. The tree of course couldn't swim at all, so it came last.

The sports' day came to an end and everyone agreed that it had been a fantastic day. Everyone that is, except for the penguin, the centipede and the rabbit. They were desperately unhappy that they had not won the events they had wanted to win.

'I was rubbish at running' moaned the penguin.

'I was rubbish at jumping' moaned the centipede.

'I was rubbish at swimming' moaned the rabbit.

No one had ever seen the penguin, centipede or rabbit unhappy, and the tree was especially upset – it hated seeing its friends so miserable.

'But you were brilliant at swimming!' it enthused to the penguin. 'Look, you won!' it added, pointing at the gold medal hanging round the penguin's neck.

'So I did' said the penguin, and he began to feel much better.

'And you were brilliant at running!' the tree likewise enthused to the centipede. 'Look, you won too!', pointing at the gold medal hanging round the centipede's neck.

'So I did' said the centipede, and he too began to feel better.

'And you rabbit, you were just brilliant at jumping!' the tree enthused yet again. 'You won *too*!', pointing at the gold medal hanging round the rabbit's neck.

'So I did' said the rabbit, and she *too* began to feel better!

'And if ever there was a 'wobbling race', you'd definitely win' said the tree, in sombre humour to the penguin. The penguin laughed, in fact they all did – 'Yes I would' he said proudly. 'I'd be the best wobbler ever!'

'And if ever there was 'wriggling like mad' event, you'd win that for sure' the tree said to the centipede.

They all laughed even more. 'Yes I would' said the centipede, as proudly as the penguin. 'I'd be the best wriggler ever!'

'And if ever there was a 'sink like a stone' event, you'd definitely win that!' the tree said to the rabbit, and they all laughed *even* more. 'Yes I would!' exclaimed the rabbit 'I'd be the best sinker ever! In fact, I'd be the *stinker* sinker!'

'You'd be the *saddest* stinker sinker!!' added the penguin.

'You'd be the *soggiest* saddest stinker sinker!!!' said the centipede, and they all collapsed in howls of uncontrollable laughter, clutching their sides and rolling around on the ground in tears. Everyone couldn't help but join in, laughing with them, and even the penguin, the centipede and the rabbit agreed – it *had* been the most fantastic day ever!

By the time the next sports' day came round, if it were possible to imagine, everyone was even more excited than in the previous year, but none more so than the penguin, the centipede, and the rabbit – the tree had given them a wonderful idea! Instead of all the usual events – running, swimming, jumping – it was announced that, this sports day would feature some very different types of event altogether: the 'Wobbling Race', followed by the 'Wriggling Like Mad' event followed by the 'Sink like a Stone' event!

The penguin, the centipede and the rabbit had a wonderful time, as they happily made complete fools of themselves, wobbling round the race track (which, of course, the centipede was rubbish at, but he tried his best!), wriggling around on the ground like mad wriggly things (which, of course the rabbit was rubbish at, but she too tried her best!) and sinking like stones, the soggier the better (which of course the penguin was rubbish at, but he *too* tried his best!)

Everyone else joined in, laughing, and kidding each other on, and once the three events were over, everyone agreed – this sports' day had been even better than the last!

The tree, as before, watched over them all, and was delighted to see its friends, and everyone else, enjoy themselves so much. It was not bothered that it could not join in like the others. What it did not know, however, was that the three friends had concocted a little surprise for their friend the tree.

'Now' they announced 'we have one more event left, the final event of the day – this is for *absolutely* everyone! It's called the 'Standing Tall' competition! Let's see, let's see - who can stand the tallest!?'

Everyone immediately tried to stand as tall as they possibly could, stretching and stretching every limb and tendon upwards as high as they were able - never had there been seen so many chins and beaks and snouts and wet noses raised so ludicrously skyward! But despite everyone's best efforts, it was easy to see who was the winner. Without even having to try, the tree towered over them all – it beamed and beamed as the gold medal was put around its neck (which took a little while, as no one had thought to bring a ladder!), and everyone clapped and cheered as the penguin, the centipede, and the rabbit proclaimed: 'The winner: our dear friend, the tree!"

For every year after that, more and more events were added to the sports day, some so ridiculous you wouldn't believe, until eventually *everyone* went home with a gold medal hanging round his or her neck!

And although the tree still couldn't join in with most of them, every year, no matter what, it would win the 'Standing Tall' event, and so effortlessly that everyone always agreed: no-one, *no-one* could ever, ever stand as tall as the tree - it clearly stood the tallest of them all!

Author's Note: Where there is paper space to do so, utilising the opportunity to present forth-coming attractions. Therefore, next, meet a sausage and an egg, who find they have much in common......

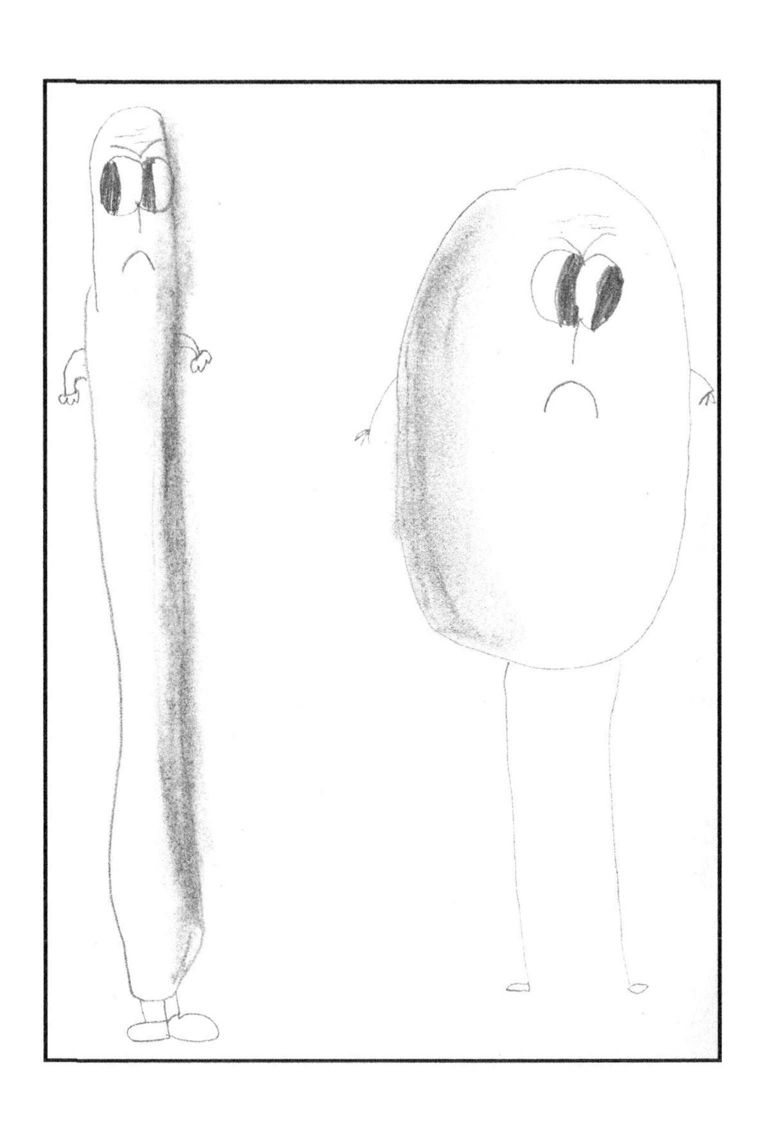

THE SAUSAGE AND THE EGG

Once upon a time there was a sausage and an egg. Both lived in a great white fridge, where they lay, quite contentedly, in the darkness beside their fellow sausages and eggs, completely oblivious of the other's existence.

Then, one day, something remarkable happened: the great white fridge door opened! A tremendous light flooded in, illuminating everything as it burst brilliantly over them. Their world changed forever! The sausage looked over at the egg, and the egg looked over at the sausage, and both were truly and utterly amazed: there's someone other than just me here, they both thought. How marvellous!

It would not be an exaggeration to say, that the two delighted *absolutely* in each others new found company, discovering such exciting things about the other that they could hardly have imagined possible!

'You're so…round!' admired the sausage of the egg.

'And you're so…straight!' admired the egg of the sausage.

'How marvellous!' they both agreed.

'And you are so…pink!' admired the egg, further of the sausage.

'And you are so…brown!' admired the sausage, further of the egg.

'How completely marvellous!' they both agreed.

'And you have a…shell?!' said the sausage, amazed, to the egg. It took some explaining on the egg's part as to what that was exactly!

'And you have a ...skin?!' said the egg to the sausage, likewise amazed! It took some explaining on the sausage's part as to what that was too!

'How wonderfully and completely marvellous!' they both agreed.

'And you have such a lovely home!' complimented the sausage to the egg, referring with genuine admiration to the pale green egg box in which the egg and his fellow eggs sat.

'As do you!' complimented the egg to the sausage, referring likewise with genuine admiration to the round white plate that the sausages lay on, all covered in layers and layers of cling film.

'How truly, wonderfully and completely marvellous!' they both agreed.

And so it was, that the sausage and the egg continued to delight in their new found friendship for some considerable time, talking every day, and sharing with each other their thoughts on just about everything, their fascination for the other and the other's world a constant source of joyful revelation.

But as time passed each began to harbour thoughts, un-nerving and disturbing thoughts, that they did not, indeed, they felt, they *could* not share - thoughts that plagued them with increasing resentment.

The sausage would look over at the egg and think: 'Why can't I have a nice warm home to sleep in? I'm left lying here, on this cold plate, no proper cover for me. It must be lovely to be so warm and protected like that. To have your own little room in your own little house. And I bet the egg gets a good night's sleep! How am I meant to, with that light waking me up all the time?' He would look at his fellow sausages, all squashed up together and think bitterly: 'I wish I were an egg.'

And the egg would look over at the sausage and think: 'Why can't I be allowed to be left out in the open? I'm always stuck here in the dark, stuck in this tiny little room, nothing to look at and no one else to talk to. It's so lonely.' He would look at his fellow eggs, all sleeping silently in their own tiny little rooms, and think bitterly: 'I wish I were a sausage.'

And the sausage would look at the egg and think: 'It must be nice to have a shell, to keep you safe like that. I've only got this thin skin. It's rubbish! I wish I were an egg.'

And the egg would look at the sausage and think: 'It must be nice to have a skin. I hate this shell - always worrying whether it's going to crack, and it's *so*... restrictive! It's rubbish! I wish I were a sausage.'

And the sausage would think: 'It must be nice to be round – I hate being long and thin. I wish *I* were an egg!'

And the egg would think: 'It must be nice to be long and thin – I hate being round. I wish *I* were a sausage!'

And the sausage would think: 'I hate being pink – I wish I was brown. I wish, I *wish* I were an egg!!'

And the egg would think: 'I hate being brown – I wish I was pink. I wish, I *wish* I were a sausage!!'

The resentment between the two grew and grew, until eventually they found that they could hardly talk to each other at all any more. Finally they lay, in complete and utter silence, confused and stubbornly ignoring the other, each in a bitter huff.

Then, one day, the fridge door opened, and the egg and sausage watched in horror as a fellow egg and sausage were lifted from their homes, and thrown, respectively, into a pot of steaming, boiling water and a pan of hot smouldering oil!

From that day forward the egg decided that it wasn't so bad being an egg, and the sausage decided that it wasn't so bad being a sausage, and they both lived contentedly and happy in each other's company (until, of course, the day came when they too were thrown to their own grim[m] fate!)

Author's Note: Next, welcome, a lonely shadow......

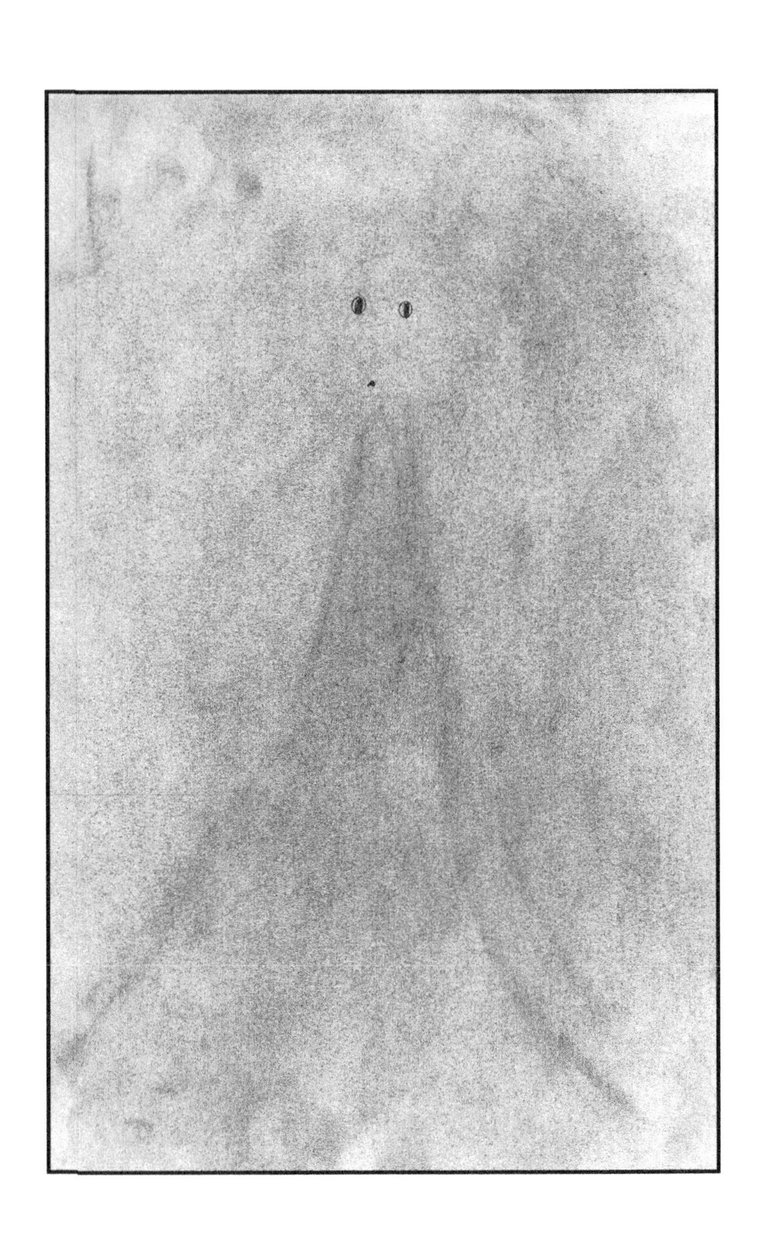

A SHADOW IN THE DARK

Once upon a time there was a shadow that lay in the dark. The shadow had no idea where it lay, nor even for that matter, how long it had lain there – all it had ever known was darkness, darkness all around, everywhere, endless and forever.

It was such a barren, lonely existence, that the shadow could not help but lament its sorry state – imagine, a shadow, in the dark? Inevitably, questions plagued the shadow, questions that would not rest, being inherently without resolution, rendering the shadow hopelessly beleaguered.

'What am I?' it would ask itself, pitifully over and over. 'What am I meant to be?'

The shadow was unable to resist some insistent sense of pertinent necessity to its being, impossible to ignore and yet impossible to define. It was a source of constant distress: and so the shadow lay, helpless, and desperately frustrated, in the impenetrable and empty darkness, without the solace of even a confidant in whom to share its terrible woe.

And then, suddenly, from somewhere high, high above, a great light appeared, washing completely the darkness away! The shadow, in an ecstatic joy, realised at last what it was, its true state revealed and with it, its true purpose.

Other shadows lay all around, all sharing in the same universal joy, and they danced the steady tender dance that only shadows can, in the pale and yet glorious, illumination!

When the darkness descended once again, the shadow was overcome by a profound and unfathomable sadness. It longed for the wondrous light to re-appear, as did its fellow shadows, and they lay together, side by side, comforting each other in their mutual yearning.

And the questions that had so plagued the shadow were at last forgotten, as it lay, waiting, in distracted expectation, for the time when it would, once again, dance in the moonlight.

Author's Note: Introducing…the two farms!

A TALE OF TWO FARMS

Once upon a time there were two farms. Life on the farms was tough, and the animals on both farms had to work very hard. Whenever there was a holiday (which wasn't very often) the animals, being so exhausted, usually just rested. Rarely, if ever, would they have the energy to play, and if they did, they would always play by themselves – it never occurred to them to play together! However, on this particular holiday, the animals on each farm had decided, quite by chance, that it might be fun if they *did* play together for a change.

On the first farm, the pig, the cow, the horse and the chicken gathered together and tried to decide what it was they wanted to do. As they had never done this before they had no idea where to start, so they ended up standing around for ages, in an awkward silence, shuffling their various hooves (or in the chickens case, scrawny claws), and staring hopelessly at the ground.

Eventually, the pig made a suggestion.

'I know! I know!' she suddenly oinked, excitedly. The others looked up with eager anticipation. 'We could all roll around in the mud!'

The other animals all groaned.

'Not I' mooed the cow. 'Disgusting!'

'Not I' neighed the horse. 'Filthy!'

'Not I' clucked the chicken. 'Yuck!'

The pig was upset that no-one liked her idea, so she went off and rolled around in the mud anyway. The others looked on, but as it really wasn't their thing, they were all very bored.

It was the cow, then, who made the next suggestion.

'I know! I know!' she mooed, excitedly. The others looked up, again, with eager and hopeful anticipation. 'We could all chew grass!'

The other animals all groaned.

'Not I' neighed the horse. 'Disgusting!'

'Not I' clucked the chicken. 'Filthy!'

'Not I' oinked the pig. 'Yuucck!!'

The cow was upset that no-one liked her idea, so she went off and chewed grass anyway. The others looked on, but as it really wasn't their thing either, they were all very, very bored.

It was then the horse who made the next suggestion.

'I know! I know!' she neighed, excitedly. The others looked up, still with a degree of hope, but their enthusiasm was clearly waning. 'We could all eat hay!'

The other animals all groaned.

'Not I' clucked the chicken. 'Disgusting!'

'Not I' oinked the pig. 'Filthy!'

'Not I' mooed the cow. 'Yuuuccck!!!'

The horse was upset that no-one liked her idea, so she went off and ate hay anyway. The others looked on, but as it really wasn't their thing either, they were all so very, *very* bored.

It was the chicken who then made the next suggestion.

'I know! I know!' she clucked, excitedly. The others looked up, but with little, if any, enthusiasm whatsoever. 'We could all lay eggs!'

The others all looked at each other – 'eh? what?' - before groaning.

'Not I' oinked the pig. 'Disgusting!'

'Not I' mooed the cow. 'Filthy!'

'Not I' neighed the horse. 'Yuuuucccck!!!!'

The chicken was upset that no-one liked her idea, so she too went off and laid eggs anyway. The others looked on (even though they didn't particularly want to!), but as it really, *really* wasn't their thing, they were all *soooo* very, *very* bored.

Finally the day came to an end, and the animals on the first farm agreed: it had been the worst day off ever! They went back to their individual pends, having already decided that if they ever had a day off again they wouldn't waste it the way they had wasted it today. Playing together was no fun at all!

On the second farm, on the other hand, the pig, the cow, the horse and the chicken had had a fantastic time! They had decided that it might be fun to form a band. None of them could sing of course, not really, but they thought, why not give it a go? We can all make noises of one sort or another, and at least it would be better than rolling in the mud, or chewing grass, or eating hay, or laying eggs – they did that every day!

So they wrote a song called 'The Farm Animal Song' which went like this:

Moo Moo Cluck Cluck Oink Oink NEEEIGGHHH!!
Moo Moo Cluck Cluck Oink Oink NEEEIGGHHH!!
Moo Moo Cluck Cluck Oink Oink NEEEIGGHHH!!
Moo Moo Cluck Cluck Oink Oink NEEEIGGHHH!!

Admittedly it was a tad repetitive, but they absolutely loved singing it! Everyone had their own part, and they would all join in with complete abandon, singing it over and over the whole day long.

Coincidentally, it so happened that an internationally famous record producer was holidaying near the farm. As he drove by in his open top stretch pink limousine, all sunglasses and chunky gold jewellery, he heard the animals giving a typically enthusiastic rendition of their song, and he was mightily impressed.

'Nevah 'ave ah heaarrrd such an awesome melodeeeh!' he drawled in his thick American accent, 'Y'all ar' gonna be superstars!', and he gave them a one million dollar recording contract right there and then!

And so it came to pass that the animals on the first farm all went to bed that night miserable and fed up, with nothing to look forward to except work, work, work, whilst all the animals on the second farm went to bed dreaming of the exciting future that awaited them: as international singing sensations – a future in which they had absolutely no doubt they would live, the rock'n'roll life......happily ever after!

Author's Note: ...a frustrated roll...

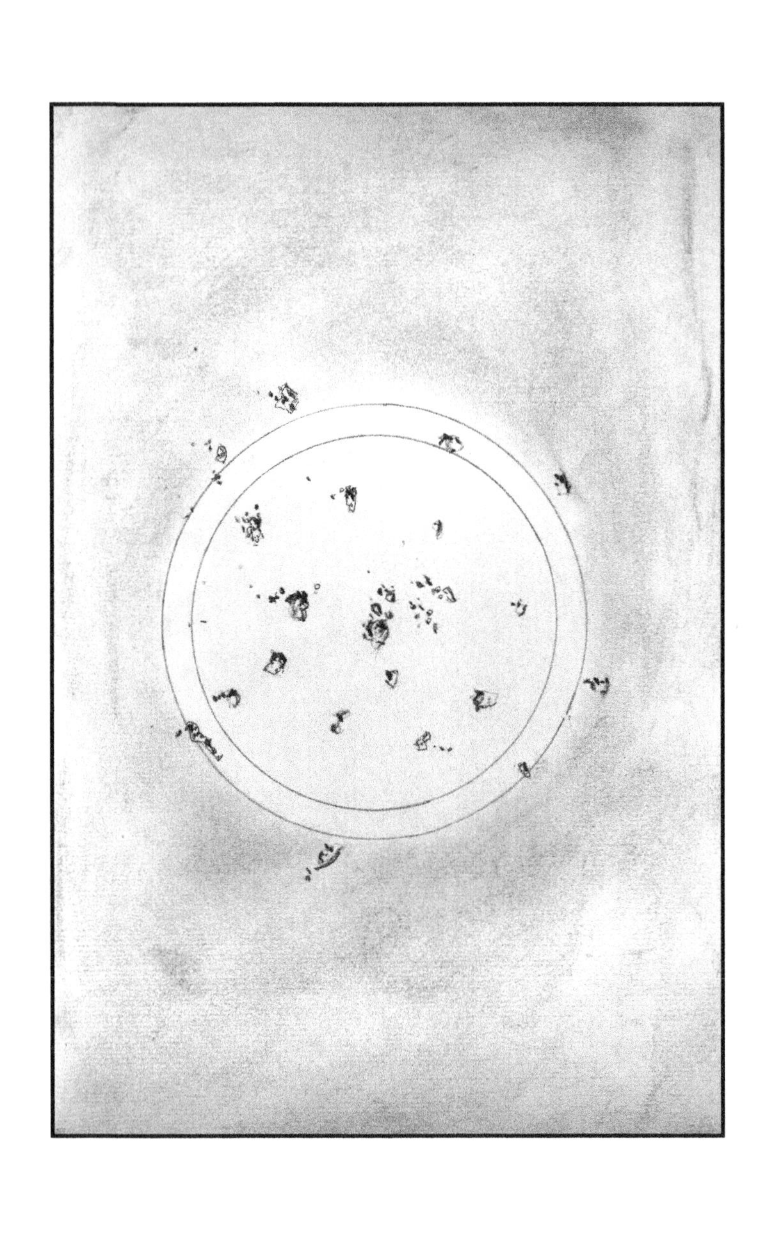

THE ROLL THAT HAD NO BACON

Once upon a time there was a roll, and it was a very, very unhappy roll. 'I want bacon' it demanded, to anyone who would listen. 'I want bacon!'

Unfortunately there wasn't any bacon, but regardless, the roll, ignoring this undeniable impediment, continued its mournful lament: 'I want bacon! I want bacon!' it insisted, over and over.

The other condiments felt sorry for the roll, and tried to help.

'How about jam instead?' suggested the jam. 'A lovely jam roll?'

'No' said the roll. 'I want bacon!'

'How about marmalade?' suggested the marmalade. 'A lovely marmalade roll?'

'NO' repeated the roll, emphatically. 'I want bacon!'

'How about honey?' said the honey. 'A lovely honey roll?'

'NO!' the roll retorted rather abruptly, beginning to raise its voice. 'I want BACON!'

Even the dairy products and the other meats tried to help.

'How about cheese?' suggested the cheese. 'A lovely cheese roll?'

'NO! NO!' snapped the roll. If it had feet it would have stamped them, so frustrated was the roll becoming. 'I WANT BACON!!'

'How about ham?' suggested the ham. 'A lovely ham roll?'

'NO! NO! NO!' shouted the roll, its impatience finally erupting. 'I WANT BACON!!!'

'How about sausage?' suggested the sausage. The sausage thought it would have the last word – surely – 'a lovely roll and sausage?' But the roll clearly did not agree: 'NO! NO! NO! NO! NO!' it screamed, hysterically. 'ARE YOU ALL DEAF!? I WANT BACON!!!!!!!!!! BACON! BACON!! BACON!!!'

Feeling that they had done their best to offer an alternative, all the condiments, dairy products and meats decided that there was nothing else for it – they would simply *have* to find some bacon for the roll, as it was quite obvious nothing else would suffice. They waited until night-time, when they could sneak out to the local shop (which, as you can imagine, for jam, marmalade, honey, cheese, ham and sausage, was no easy feat) to steal some bacon – yes, they were prepared to even break the law! – on the roll's behalf.

In the morning, when the roll awoke, it was overjoyed to find the bacon waiting for it. The other condiments, dairy products and meats had been rather nervous that the roll might have changed its mind, and they'd stayed up for the whole remainder of the night, unable to sleep, waiting and watching for the roll to wake up. So they too were overjoyed, as much out of relief as anything, that the roll was happy, and, all credit to the roll, it was not slow to acknowledge their generous efforts.

'I'm sorry' it said to the jam, the marmalade, the honey, the cheese, the ham, and the sausage in turn, rather shamefully.

'That's alright' they replied, bleary eyed and yawning. 'You enjoy your bacon' they said, before retiring to bed for a well deserved nap.

When they awoke, later that day, the roll and bacon was nowhere to be found. Only a few crumbs remained on the plate where it had last been seen. It was quite apparent what had happened - the roll had been eaten!

'Shame' they said to each other, but secretly they were rather delighted – all that miserable roll did all day was moan-bloody-moan!

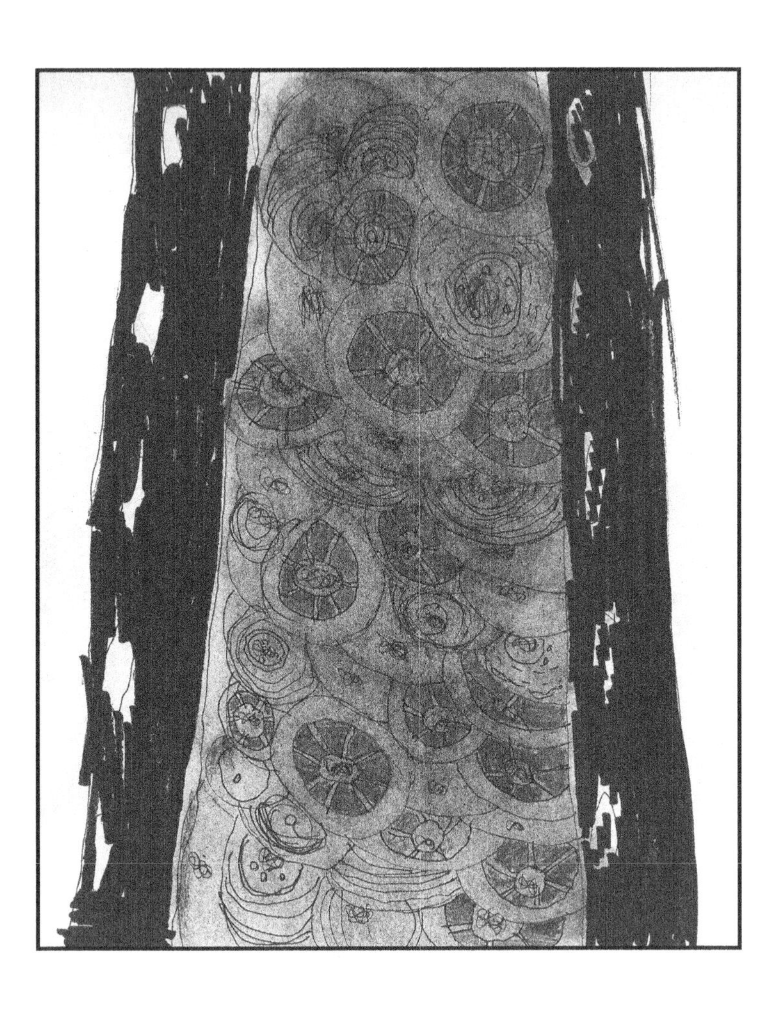

THE CAR THAT HAD NO WHEEL

Once upon a time there was a car that had no wheel. The car sat, immobile and alone, in the forecourt of a vacant and dilapidated old garage, its missing wheel propped up unsteadily on a pile of broken bricks and stones.

How long the car had been sitting like that it did not know. All it did know was that it felt like it had been sitting there *forever*. If the car's condition was anything to go by, this would certainly seem to be not terribly far from the truth – its once fine coat, from the car's own dim recollection a beautifully bright shade of sky blue, was now sadly flaked and rusted away, its windows, those that were left, blinded by dust, and its luxurious leather upholstery was all torn and burst. The tyres on its remaining three wheels were completely flat, cobwebs were everywhere, and small animals had even taken to nesting in its engine! All its oil, water and fuel had completely dried up, its lights were broken and smashed, and as for its wipers, mirrors, hubcaps, those little pieces of necessity and finery that any car might take for granted, well, who knew where they were? Perhaps lying amongst the other junk that surrounded the car, the countless empty paint pots and smelly oil cans, broken tools fallen from overturned work benches, splintered and discarded pallets, rotting cardboard boxes and other rusting bits of twisted metal and machinery.

All in all, it was a lame and redundant sight – hardly could one picture a car more abandoned than this. It was not particularly surprising therefore that the car was somewhat depressed.

'I'm not meant to be here' it thought, perpetually and sullenly to itself. 'I should be over there.'

The 'there' to which the car was referring was the freeway, miles off, where all manner of vehicles could be seen hurtling along, this way and that, endlessly, day and night. The blue car couldn't begin to measure the envy it felt for those other vehicles, all those cars, and vans, trucks, and buses, even the motor bikes! Every single one of them: they were free to do what they wanted, free to roam, as fast or as slowly as they liked, wherever and whenever, free, free to be what they were meant to be: free to drive! It was something that was so simple, so fundamental for every vehicle, all because they had a full complement of that most critical necessity of all – wheels. And here this blue car was, short of just one, and it couldn't do a thing. Not a thing, other than to just sit and stare, as it rusted slowly away, its memories of driving, fading to the point where the car could hardly remember the feeling at all.

It wasn't even as if the blue car had anyone to accompany it in its empty vigil - it had no-one to talk to, no-one to share its sadness with, no one. The derelict garage sat on the edge of a lonely little country road, itself overrun with bracken and refuse. Hardly anyone ever drove down it, and even if the occasional vehicle did come along, would it ever stop? Well, why would it? The pumps, like the car's engine, were all dried up; there was no fuel, no shop, nothing. And why would any other car want to sit and listen to this blue car's pathetic tale of woe?

So the blue car would sit and stare, hour after hour, day after day, month after month, at the freeway in the distance, wishing without hope for something it could hardly even put into words.

Then, one day, as the blue car was dozing in the heat of the early afternoon sun, a little red sports car pulled up in front of the derelict garage. It had to wake the blue car from its slumbers, revving its engine, and gently pumping its sweet horn.

'Hello' said the little red car in a bright and pleasant voice, as the blue car, startled from its sleep, rubbed its eyes, and tried to focus.

'Hello', it eventually croaked in reply. It had been a long time since the blue car had talked to anyone – its voice was as cracked and rusty as its bodywork!

'I wonder if you could help me?' said the red car, once the blue car had coughed and cleared its throat a little. 'I seem to be a little lost. Sorry if I woke you.'

'Lost?' queried the blue car.

'Yes, lost' repeated the red car. 'I was on the freeway, but I think I took a wrong exit.'

'Where do you want to get to?' asked the blue car, still struggling to speak clearly. It coughed again, as it thought to itself: it couldn't be to anywhere near here. No-one ever wants to come here. As it suspected, the little red car said: 'I really just want to get back to the freeway. Do you know the way?'

'Just follow the road round' answered the blue car, with a morose nod of its broken headlights. 'Don't worry – it'll take you straight there, straight back onto the freeway', it added, morosely still and not without some degree of jealous envy in its voice.

The red car didn't seem to notice. 'Thank you, thank you ever so much' it gratefully replied in its own cheerful, sunny voice.

The blue car wished the red car would stay. It was such a beautiful little sports car – it would love to hear stories of where it had been, what it had seen, maybe even just to be reminded of what it felt like to drive again, even if the memory would doubtless make it somewhat saddened by the recollection. Or even if the red car would just sit, even for a little while – it was so desperately lonely. But the blue car simply couldn't bring itself to ask, couldn't bring itself to impose on anyone else, especially such a beautiful little car as this, a car which almost certainly would have much better places to be than here, and have much more interesting things to do and friends to talk to. Why would any car, especially this beautiful little thing, be the slightest bit interested in staying?

But, much to the blue car's surprise, the red car did not just drive off as expected. It continued to sit there, looking at the blue car, a kind and caring, if slightly quizzical, expression on its face.

'Sorry, but are you alright? You seem a little down' it asked.

The blue car didn't know what to say – it was such an unlikely thing to be asked, and after so long, waiting, it took the blue car completely off guard. The last thing it wanted was for the little red car to think it was as pathetic as it felt.

'Oh. I'm alright' said the blue car, feigning nonchalance that, truly, it did not feel. 'Just, you know, resting up a wee bit, you know.'

'OK', said the red car, unconvinced, 'you sure?'

'Sure' said the blue car, bluffing as jovially as it could. 'Catching some rays, that's all.'

The red car still didn't move – it looked at the blue car with such a consideration that the blue car began to feel uncomfortable. Eventually it asked:

'What happened to your wheel? Do you mind me asking?'

The blue car should have been embarrassed, but the red car seemed so genuinely concerned, and it was such a delightful little thing after all, that the blue car couldn't help but be seduced into feeling comfortable in confiding: 'Actually, I don't know. I can't really remember. It's been like that for so long. I can't remember a time when it wasn't, actually.... well, almost.'

'Oh, but that's terrible' sympathised the red car, with heartfelt sincerity. 'That is so awful for you.'

The blue car tried to be casual about it, and, pretending to be much braver than it actually felt, said: 'I don't mind. I've got used to it.'

'Oh, but you shouldn't. You really shouldn't. If it was me, I'd mind terribly. I don't know how you can bear it.' The red car was clearly shocked.

'You *do* get used to it' the blue car lied.

'Well that's not right. No car should have to put up with something like this' insisted the red car. It paused for a minute.

'Listen, I tell you what' it continued, 'you can borrow my wheel for a while if you like.'

'Borrow your wheel?' The blue car could hardly contain its incredulity. 'Really?'

The red car hesitated, but only a little, before saying decisively 'Sure. Sure you can.'

The blue car was almost dumbstruck. A chance to drive again – it was unbelievable!

'But – I couldn't...I mean. I don't know if I can. And I'm all broken ...I don't even have fuel or anything.'

'Oh, don't worry about that – you can have some of mine. We'll soon get you sorted out. I'll come by tomorrow and let you have a go.'

Suddenly the blue car didn't believe the little red car any more. Come back tomorrow? That'd be likely! The red car just wanted to get away, like everyone else. Who could blame it? But the blue car felt angry nonetheless, at the red car for leading it on - how cruel! It wouldn't be back, and the blue car knew it, and knew that the red car knew it too. It turned its face away, bitterly hurt.

The red car flashed its little lights at the blue car – 'I promise' it said. The blue car ignored it and said nothing, as the little red car disappeared down the road and out of sight around the bend.

All night the blue car tried to sleep, but it couldn't. It kept having the same awful dream, over and over. At first, everything in the dream was wonderful – the blue car was no longer a rusting wreck, but instead, as good as new, shining blue, with no broken parts, and no missing wheel! It dreamt that it was hurtling along the freeway, faster and faster and faster. How truly amazing it felt, as it sped along, and as it did so, its whole body was transformed; every single part of the car, all its bodywork, its engine, its interior, its seats, everything became glass, vibrant shades of coloured glass! Sunlight shone through it, casting glorious rainbow patterns across the freeway, and over, too, all the other vehicles that lined the edge of the freeway. They sat side by side all along the hard shoulder, thousands and thousands of them, flashing their lights and pumping their horns, cheering the blue car on as it sped by.

But as the blue car got faster, so fast in fact that it became almost a blur, its tyres gradually began to heat up. They got hotter and hotter, and hotter still, until they began to actually melt! Suddenly the blue car was in agony. The pain was unbelievable. Its tyres began to burn, and were torn bit by bit from its wheels, leaving pieces of smouldering rubber all along the freeway.

The blue car, its four wheels now completely ablaze, screamed to the other cars, to please help, please, please, to put out the terrible fires, but they just kept on cheering, flashing their lights and sounding their horns, louder and louder. Eventually all the tyres were completely burnt off, and yet still the blue car did not stop – it sped on, faster and faster, its wheels screeching along the freeway in a torrent of sparks. Every bump in the road caused the car to jolt brutally and with an ever increasing intensity, continually shaking the car in even greater agony. Horrendous cracks opened up, everywhere, great ragged cracks that criss-crossed the whole of the blue car's body, until finally, with one last terrible shudder, the car shattered into thousands and thousands of shards of broken glass that exploded all across the freeway!

It was a miserable night, and when in the morning the blue car finally awoke, it was bloodshot and weary. Never had it felt so bad, or so keenly unhappy, as it did then. It was certainly therefore not feeling anything near its best when the little red car re-appeared around the bend.

'See, I told you I'd be back' it said cheerily, as it pulled up again in front of the garage.

The blue car couldn't help itself: 'I thought you wouldn't come', it said, gruffly, unable to dispel its sullen huff, despite being, in truth, happier than it could ever remember.

'A promise is a promise' replied the red car earnestly.

The blue car, if it could, would have cried buckets. As it was, it could only rattle its rusty body instead, suddenly shaking all over, uncontrollably.

'Now, now, come on, cheer up' consoled the red car. It flashed its little lights at the blue car, which began slowly to calm down. 'Come on' it said again, encouragingly, once the blue car had fully collected itself. 'Let's get this show on the road!'

Being true to its word, the red car passed one of its wheels to the blue car. It took a while for the blue car to get used to it, but slowly everything came back, and the blue car soon felt confident enough to go for a drive.

'You go off and enjoy yourself' said the red car, its own missing wheel now propped up on the same pile of broken bricks and stones.

'Oh I will! I will!' said the blue car, almost giddy with joy, as it began to head off down the road.

'And don't forget about me' the red car shouted after it.

'I won't' the blue car shouted back.

'You promise?'

'I promise'.

And with that the blue car disappeared round the bend. The red car looked over at the freeway in the distance, and settled down patiently to wait until the blue car returned.

By the time the blue car reached the freeway, it had completely mastered the new wheel. Driving felt just as exhilarating as the blue car remembered – free at last! Free to go wherever it chose. It was wonderful!

Taking all the twists and turns in the little country roads had really been something, but nothing compared to the excitement of the freeway itself. My, oh my, the speed! The blue car could hardly contain itself, as it raced, faster and faster, shouting out ludicrously joyful greetings to every vehicle it passed. They in turn could only look back in a confused humour – clearly someone was on something! That high octane fuel no doubt?!

The day wore on, and the blue car completely lost track of time, and distance, for that matter. 'I'd better get back' it eventually said to itself, as dusk began to settle. But it suddenly realised that it was completely lost. It asked everyone if they knew the way back to the little country road and the old garage, but no-one knew what it was talking about.

'I'll try again tomorrow' the blue car said to itself, somewhat upset at not being able to return the wheel to the little red car, but still so overjoyed from its amazing day to counter any real feelings of regret. 'The red car will be ok for one night' it re-assured itself. 'I'll get back tomorrow.'

But when tomorrow came, again, the blue car could not find its way back. In truth it knew that it didn't really try. 'Just one more day' it told itself. 'The red car won't mind if I take just one more day'. No-one seemed to know how to get back to the garage anyway, maybe tomorrow. So the blue car had another wonderful day, and yet another, racing along the freeway, making lots and lots of new friends.

And so it went on, day after day, the blue car making endless excuses to itself, convincing itself that the red car would not mind just another day – after all, the blue car had sat without *its* wheel for many, many more days than that!

Day after day, and every day the blue car made more friends, and discovered more and more wonderful things that it had forgotten – especially those things that were on offer at the service stations! Oh, the wonder of the car wash, for example, goodness, how amazing was that, or how amazing it was to fill up with fuel, or have its tyres pumped up! It was all so incredible! And bit by bit, the blue car even had its bodywork repaired, all its broken parts were gradually renewed, its engine fixed, all its windows replaced, its lights too – everything, until it was once again the beautiful blue car of old!

Eventually, as the days turned into weeks, and the weeks into months, the blue car forgot about the little red car. Except, that is, when it would pass an abandoned car on the hard shoulder - there were a few, now and again. Pathetic they were, sitting there, with a wheel missing, and nothing to do but whine at the passing cars and other vehicles. So his friends would say, and the blue car would feign agreement, although it would always, even if just momentarily, be reminded of the red car that it had left similarly abandoned at the old garage. But the blue car told no-one about the red car, and assuaged its guilt by telling itself how very unlikely it was that the red car would still be there. Doubtless someone would have come along by now, someone would surely have offered a wheel to the red car, as the red car had offered one to the blue car. That *surely* would be the case. And so the blue car finally convinced itself, and did completely forget all about the little red car.

Many, many years passed, and life for the blue car was grand – it had everything that it could possibly want.

Everything, that is, except recently and more so every day, it appeared to have fewer and fewer friends to run with.

'What's happened to so-and-so?' had become a staple aspect of conversation amongst the blue car and its friends.

'Haven't seen so-and-so for ages,' was the common reply. 'Wonder what happened?' No-one ever seemed to know, it was very unusual, and was it just coincidence, or where there more abandoned cars by the side of the freeway? The blue car couldn't be sure, could it be......?

One day the blue car came across one of his friends, sitting all alone on the hard shoulder.

'Hi there' the blue car greeted his friend enthusiastically. 'Fancy going for a run?'

His friend looked back, glumly. 'I can't' it said, nodding to its missing back wheel.

'Oh' said the blue car, not knowing what to say.

'But once I get this fixed I'll be right with you' said its friend optimistically.

'Sure, sure' humoured the blue car. 'Sure – well, see you.' The blue car couldn't get away fast enough.

From that day on the blue car seemed to meet more and more of its friends, similarly abandoned with a wheel or two missing. It became quite awful – at first the blue car would stop to talk, but eventually it just sped by, ignoring them, and their almost desperate pleas for help. 'What can I do?' it would say to itself, and went about its daily business, trying to disregard the ever increasing numbers of derelict cars sitting on the hard shoulder.

Maintaining its lifestyle was, however, becoming more and more difficult for the blue car. One day, a car wash closed, some time after that a body shop. Then a whole service station shut down. The blue car had to travel further and further to find fuel, and slowly its bodywork began to suffer. Little scratches could not be mended any more, bigger dents could not be beaten out, there was no-one left to do the repairs. Ever so slowly the blue car's fine coat began to rust. It would normally have been embarrassed to be seen in such a shabby condition, but by way of small consolation, there were clearly fewer and fewer vehicles on the roads anyway. Sometimes for days on end, the blue car wouldn't pass anyone at all – although he needn't have felt lonely, there were always plenty of cars abandoned on the hard shoulder. More and more and more of them.

At last the blue car could not stand it any longer, driving endlessly along the empty freeway, and being constantly stared at, imploringly, by vehicles that now seemed to line the freeway no matter where it went. It decided that anything was better than this, and so it took the next exit and headed off down into the country roads. It couldn't go nearly as fast, but at least it didn't have to deal with all those bleak and forlorn stares!

Having to take the sharp twists and turns of the country roads soon made the blue car realise what a state it had become. It seriously needed an oil change, could certainly do with some new tyres for sure, and its brakes – goodness, they were just shot! Most worrying of all however was the lack of fuel – and not a garage in sight! It was with some relief therefore that, as the blue car turned one of the typically sharp bends, a garage came into view!

The blue car's relief was immediately dispelled however – this wasn't just any garage. It was *the* garage, the same garage where it had spent all those years, neglected and alone, the same garage where it had left, abandoned, the little red car.

Crawling up as slowly as it could towards the garage, the blue car desperately hoped the red car was gone. Surely it must be. But no – there the red car was, just as the blue car had left it, propped up on the same sad pile of bricks and stones. Actually, at first the blue car wasn't entirely sure – was this really the same car? Its colour was nearly gone, it was rusted everywhere, all its lights broken, windows smashed – it was in a terrible condition! The blue car could hardly believe it, but as it came closer, it saw, without any doubt, that it was in fact the same car. 'Could I have been such a mess too, at one time?' it asked itself, suddenly terribly ashamed. 'What have I done?'

The shame and remorse were almost overwhelming, and it longed to just turn around, and head back in the other direction – but there was not nearly enough room to do so. It had no choice, but to continue.

However, as the blue car came closer to the garage, it realised that the red car appeared to be sleeping!

'Oh, thank goodness', thought the blue car, and it inched its way past as silently as it could, trying to avoid wakening the little red car. It had nearly reached the far side of the garage when a quiet and fragile voice said: 'I knew you'd come back.'

The blue car stopped – again, it wondered: could this really be the same little red car? Its voice had been so cheerful, and so full of life. This voice was terribly, terribly weak, and so… hollow, almost broken.

'I knew it' the red car said again, more, it seemed, to itself than to anyone else. The blue car could only stare.

'I...' it began. 'I don't know what to say' was the best it could do. It hung its head. 'I'm sorry. I'm sorry I was away for so long.'

'You don't need to be sorry, I understand. It must have been quite wonderful?' said the red car. The blue car still didn't know what to say. It couldn't bring itself to even look at the red car.

'You don't need to be so sad' urged the red car. 'You can borrow my wheel again you know, if you want', it added.

The blue car looked up. The little red car was looking back at it, openly, with not the slightest air of admonishment in either its gaze or its voice. What shame the blue car had felt evaporated, to be replaced by a sense of utter worthlessness that it could hardly comprehend.

After what seemed like an eternity and with a finality that even the little red car could find no words to counter, the blue car said: 'I don't deserve this', and silently it returned the borrowed wheel.

'Thank you' said the little red car, once its wheel was re-attached. The blue car said nothing, still unable to return the red car's considerate gaze, only looking up once it heard the red car turn and drive away. It watched in silence as the red car disappeared down the road. And then, just as it was about to limp out of sight around the bend, the red car stopped. Turning back to the blue car, it called out: 'Thank you. Thank you for keeping your promise.'

The blue car sat, once again, all alone, in the forecourt of the dilapidated old garage propped up unsteadily on the pile of broken bricks and stones. Day and night the car had nothing else to do but sit and stare, stare, at the freeway in the distance. It longed to see the freeway as it had once been, to see all those cars and trucks and buses, all those thousands and thousands of other vehicles, endlessly hurtling along it, hurtling this way and that, as they had done so in the past. But it couldn't, as nothing there now moved. Nothing. Nothing at all.

THE HOTEL THAT HAD NO BEDS

Once upon a time there was a hotel that had no beds. One might think that a hotel with such a fundamental impediment would not fare particularly well, would not presumably, be particularly popular.

But this was not, in fact, the case – this hotel was actually *the* most popular in the whole country! Every room was reserved, every night of every year. Guests, evidently, did not seem to mind that there were no beds – because they all brought their own!

One could not fail to find the hotel therefore – all one had to do was look out for the long queue of guests that stretched from the hotel reception, through the grand portico, down the long winding drive, and out onto the street, a whole multitude of guests, all lined up beside their beds. They brought every type of bed imaginable: from great four posters, carved, ornate and flattered in velvet drapes to confounding collapsible canvas carry cots; from insipid grey and too high sided hospital beds bound in starched and rigid sheets to all manner of brightly coloured sleeping bags; from adults only queen-sized and king-sized beds to miniature children's beds and heirloom baby cribs; from brass beds to wooden beds to metal beds to water beds, to a bed, once, that was even made of ice!

The queue would stretch for miles – miles and miles, of people and their beds, and others too, those who couldn't actually bring a bed, who might have strapped mattresses to their backs, or gathered together random assortments of sheets, blankets and pillows. And then there were those who couldn't afford to bring items of such nominal comfort as these, those who just gathered up anything they could find – odd bits of cardboard, discarded newspapers, even twigs or rotting damp leaves, anything, anything at all that they might use, upon which they might rest, in order to have the opportunity of staying at the hotel with no beds.

And why then, why was it, that a hotel such as this *was* so popular? Well, it was simply, that, in every other regard, apart from the lack of beds, the hotel was...... *perfect*!

From its remarkable location, with the most stunning of views through its grand windows of loch, mountains and sky; its restaurant menu, with every kind of cuisine one could possibly want or imagine, cooked to one's exact taste; its décor and associated ambience throughout the reception rooms, and the rooms themselves (rooms, as they were called – not bedrooms of course!), all so delightfully composed and of unbelievable luxury and grandeur; and then there was the staff: from porter to receptionist to waiter to masseur to chef; from the manger – *(ooopps, sorry, genuine typo!)* - the *manager* to the maid, none could be kinder, more receptive, accommodating and generous in the service that they provided.

It was without question the most perfect hotel imaginable. Not one single guest, not one ever, had cause to make a complaint. Not one. And every guest who stayed always had *the* most perfect night's sleep that they could ever, ever, *ever* recall!

Not bad, for a hotel, with no beds!

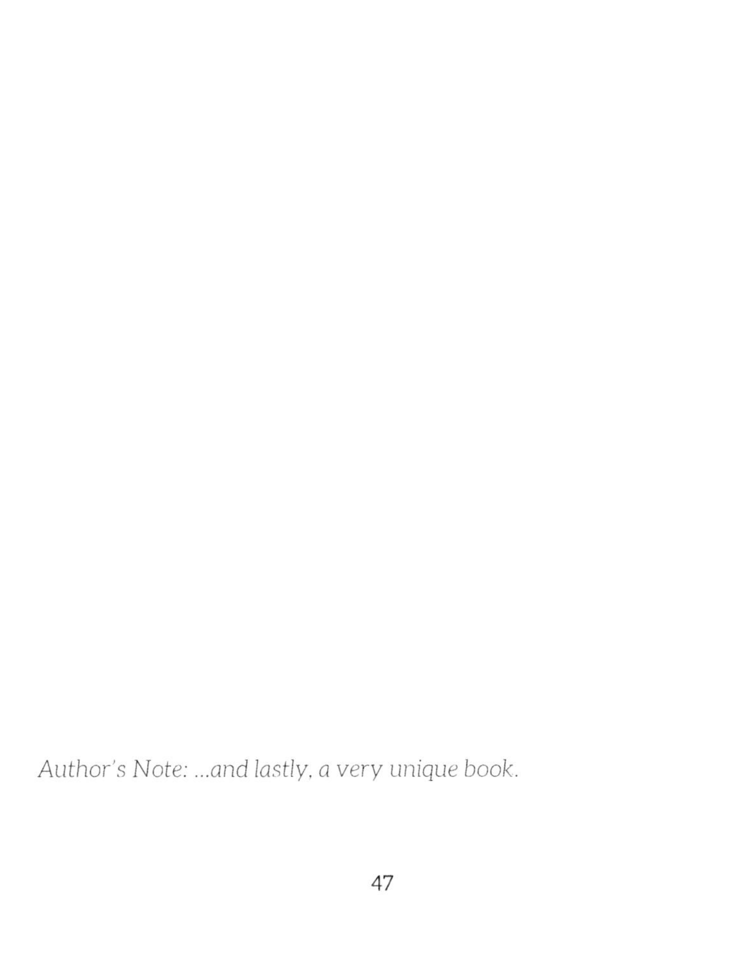

Author's Note: ...and lastly, a very unique book.

THE BOOK THAT HAD NO WORDS

Once upon a time, there was a book that had no words. All the other books would laugh at the book, teasing and mocking it, over and over – 'imagine' they'd say, 'a book with no words? What use is that? You're the worst book ever!'

But the book never appeared bothered by the endless tirade of abuse hurled at it, content it seemed, to simply ignore the hurtful comments. Not once did it even attempt to defend itself!

Eventually the abuse stopped, the other books having exhausted their capacity to verbalise their disgust, preferring instead to ignore the book, in contempt as much for its lack of character as for its lack of content. It was truly, in their opinion, a pathetic excuse of a book, spineless, not even worthy of derision.

What they did not know was that the book, although bereft of words, was instead full of pictures, as many pictures as the other books had words, and as the book without words knew very well, every picture is worth a thousand words.......

Author's Note: An apology to the reader, for the shortness of this short, short story - brevity was, understandably, considered to be both necessary and appropriate!

THE LIGHTHOUSE THAT HAD NO LIGHT

"Give light, and the darkness will disappear of itself."
ERASMUS, DESIDERIUS

Once upon a time there was a lighthouse, which had no light. If viewed from afar, it would appear to be an exceptionally handsome lighthouse, standing tall and slender on a rocky promontory, confronting the sea with such apparent confidence and purpose. But, if one were to come closer, one would soon see that in fact the lighthouse was rather old, old, and rather neglected: its white paint, which from distance seemed dazzling and luminously bright, was all washed out and everywhere flaking off; its thick and heavy wooden door, which should have been soundly and firmly closed against the severe and brutal coastal weather, was hanging loose from corroded hinges, its lock shattered and its panels splintered and rotten; all the lighthouse's small windows were broken too, and the glass in its lantern light completely gone, leaving only the thin metal frame utterly exposed, to slowly and gradually rust away.

Inside, the wind gusted, unchallenged, up through the lighthouse's spiralling stairwell, whistling through the similarly rusted open-tread metal stairs and ornate balustrade, and swirling around the dead leaves that had gathered everywhere, their constant rustling complementing the rustling of the pages in the abandoned lighthouse log book, which fluttered and turned randomly as if read by an invisible and distracted hand. Everywhere, dark browny-red stains ran down the lighthouse walls, both inside and out, and a smell of damp and musty decay pervaded every room.

It was, all in all, a terribly sad and forlorn state for the lighthouse to be in. Only however, at night, could it be fully appreciated just how utterly neglected the lighthouse truly was, particularly if a storm raged or if one of the not uncommon heavy fogs had rolled in from the sea. The lighthouse could only stand, pathetically mute and unlit, as these elements too, along with the wind, invaded its every corner, uninhibited and likewise unchallenged, appearing to almost consume the lighthouse entirely, the lighthouse in the darkness defeated and powerless to dispel them.

So the lighthouse sat, seemingly abandoned, to perpetually waste away, battered relentlessly by the sea spray and raging winds that howled around the rocky promontory, night and day.

Nearby, in the local port, the daily business of life went on, regardless of the lighthouse plight, too overly full of its own worries and concerns to care. For the port, like the lighthouse, was also a sad and neglected place. On the long main street which faced onto the port's great harbour, only a few of its shops were occupied and still open for business. The majority were closed, boarded up and vacant. A single tavern, where once there had been many, offered solace for those who congregated to drink and smoke – those who could afford it that is. They were few but regular in number, but no fewer than those who continued to gather for the weekly service at the one remaining church, where the ongoing concern was as much the condition of the church's roof, and whether it would survive the coming winter, as it was heavenly worship.

Of the many other businesses and amenities once offered by the port, most had long since shut down or moved away. The post office diligently persisted, and what correspondence there was, forwarded by the elderly and principled post mistress with proper dedication. Dedicated too, although more out of necessity than willingness, was the young hairdresser who single-handedly managed the hairdresser's next door. The same dedication however was not apparent in the burly constable who manned the police station, or in the last remaining teacher, a thin elderly gentleman with stooped back and broken glasses, who ran the local school: they, like most of the port's dwindling inhabitants, existed without enthusiasm for any ambition, nor even purpose, other than, it seemed, to perpetuate bitterness and cynical resentment.

And that was all - all that remained of what had once been a thriving and vibrant little community. The hotel was now closed, like the shops, boarded up and often vandalised, the manor house too, the fire station, surgery - all closed. Even in the harbour itself, only a couple of small, local fishing boats sat, where once had been a whole fleet: on any given day, a whole myriad of other vessels might also have crowded the harbour; from great sailing ships and foul steamers, to yachts, schooners, tugs, trawlers, to even on occasion a splendid oil tanker or warship, which would take refuge from time to time to shelter from stormy weather and high seas. It had all been so, once upon a time, but no longer.

Conversations in the port revolved forever on times past, how much better things were then than now, sour conversations filled with acrimony and regret. Rarely, if ever, was there much opportunity for any of the port's inhabitants to get excited about anything.

Today however, today was different! The new doctor was coming to the port! It was the first newcomer for years, and so unique was this that many took it as a sign, that perhaps things might finally get better, that this might signal a new start for the port – at the very least, the surgery would be open again!

Some remnant of civic pride persuaded the port's public authorities that an official welcoming reception would be somewhat unwarranted. Indeed, it would be impossible for something so grand not to appear rather desperate and fundamentally quite undignified. In retrospect, however, such an event may have served at least a practical purpose - over the initial weeks following the doctor's arrival, just about everyone in the port found an excuse of some sort or another to make an appointment with him, in an epidemic of incurable curiosity!

It was generally agreed, although with, inevitably, some small number of detractors, that the doctor was a fine man, serious, hard working, knowledgeable and clearly committed to his profession. He was duly offered the deference that his position and carriage deserved, although those same few detractors persistently and stubbornly withheld their respect and maintained their distance.

This however, could not be said of the port's response to the doctor's daughter. She was a pale little thing, sickly pale, thin, with long and straight dark hair that framed a similarly thin and pretty face, features well defined, and eyes, of a curious grey-blue, that were most remarkable. Everyone, *everyone*, immediately liked the little girl – she was always kind-hearted and generous, and chatted happily with everyone she met, interested in everything and enthusing constantly about something or other. Her sallow pallor was soon understood to be the result of protracted illness, that still lingered and on occasion would recur, confining the little girl to bed for days on end. But this served only to endear her even more: who could not help but admire such resolution and cheerful temperament in one so small, in the face of such a debilitating complaint?

Ben, the old harbour master, in particular seemed to take a liking for the little girl, and she for him. They sat endlessly together on the harbour dockside, he making her laugh, pulling silly faces and talking in funny voices as he regaled her with sea faring tales of adventure, full of pirates and princes and far off lands. And whenever the little girl was taken ill, it was the harbour master's wife who would look after her, in the absence of her father who often worked tirelessly in the surgery downstairs. She would make up a rich, strong broth which she would feed to the little girl herself, sitting through the night with her, knitting as she slept, and comforting her when her breath failed and she was overcome in fits of painful coughing.

Some months after the new doctor's arrival, the little girl, temporarily free from the confinement of her illness, went for a walk – it was such a beautiful sunny day, and she lost all track of time, as she wandered up into the hills, through the thick forest woods that surrounded the port. She soon became quite disorientated, and increasingly afraid, as the light began to fade and it became much, much colder in the gloom of the approaching evening.

The warm summer breeze turned to an icy wind, and above her the tall trees began to sway violently as the wind strengthened. Soon it began to rain too, soaking right through the little girl's thin dress and plastering her hair all over her face. She struggled desperately through the dense undergrowth, becoming more and more frightened, the weather getting worse by the minute - but at last, at last she finally came to the edge of the forest. The port was nowhere in sight, however in the distance she could just make out the old lighthouse standing isolated on the rocky outcrop.

'I must get there' she told herself – even though it looked terribly dangerous. Huge waves were crashing against the base of the lighthouse, accompanied by tremendous cracks of thunder that broke overhead. There was no shelter anywhere between the forest and the lighthouse, and the rain and wind were gusting harder than ever. She stumbled over the rough ground, losing her shoe on one occasion, and falling on the hard rocks on another, skinning her knee quite badly. But eventually, just as night fell, she made it to the large stone steps that led up to the old lighthouse door. Pushing the broken door open, she collapsed thankfully onto the floor, shivering and soaked through.

She had only lain there for a minute, when suddenly, out of the darkness above her, a deep and angry voice shouted: 'GET OUT!' The little girl looked up, terrified, as the voice shouted again, louder to the point where the lighthouse itself seemed to shake: 'GET OUT!!!....'

In abject fear, the little girl stumbled outside, only to be hit immediately by the howling gale that raged all around. The lighthouse door slammed shut behind her.

'....and STAY OUT!'

Tears poured down the little girl's cheeks as she huddled in the doorway, trying to find what shelter she could, but it was impossible. The wind and rain lashed over her, as did the torrential waves. She sank onto the hard stone steps and lay curled up into a ball, getting colder and colder, until she began to lose consciousness in the freezing onslaught.

'Please, please let me in' she said faintly, her strength failing her, her pale cheek resting against the hard wooden door. 'Please...' she whispered.

Just as she passed out, the door opened, and she fell, limply, inside.

When the little girl awoke, the sun was shining through the small windows high in the lighthouse hall where she lay. Leaves completely covered her, a pile of which had also been formed into a kind of pillow. It might have given the little girl some cause for consideration, how the leaves came to be gathered in such fashion, but she was completely distracted by the stairwell that rose above her. She lay there for a long time, looking up at the stairs that seemed to disappear into infinity – she had never seen such a sight, and how strange and captivating it was. An endless dark spiral that went up and up and up, up to a tiny pin-point of intense, white light - a stair that led right up into the sky, perhaps, or into the clouds themselves, or even, even up to heaven itself?

The hardness of the stone floor beneath her finally roused the little girl from her day dream, and she sat up, shaking the leaves off as she did so. Her hair was still a little damp, and though her dress was dry, she was still cold. She looked around for something to wear. An old raincoat was hanging on the back of the lighthouse door – she pulled it on (it was so big it almost came to her feet!) and immediately felt much better, even though it was ripped and rather smelly.

She looked around again. It was all very quiet – the little girl wondered who had shouted at her. There didn't seem to be anyone here. Slightly nervously the little girl looked up again into the stairwell. 'Hello?' she said, quietly. Nothing. She said it again, this time a bit louder. 'Hello?' Her voice echoed back to her, but no other voice accompanied it. She tried one more time – nothing.

She still half expected the horrible voice that she'd heard the night before to shout out at her again, and part of her just wanted to run away. But somehow, somehow the lighthouse didn't seem anything like as scary as it had the night before. Perhaps it was just the daylight that helped. Perhaps it was also because she was so, so hungry, and if there was food to be found it would have to be here in the lighthouse, because there certainly wouldn't be any outside!

'There's no one here' she said firmly to herself, to re-assure herself as much as anything, and, letting her hunger feed her bravery, she resolved to explore the lighthouse, at least a little!

The metal stairs creaked and groaned alarmingly as she began to climb them, and her knee hurt dreadfully too, with every step - she hadn't noticed until then just how badly she had hurt it. Maybe she'd find some medicine or bandages somewhere. But all the rooms she looked in, and there weren't many of them, seemed to be completely empty – and they were all so tiny, so much so that the little girl wondered what on earth they could have been for! Some were hardly rooms at all, alcoves almost, that one could climb into straight from the stairs themselves. In one there was an old desk, with a broken chair and an old phone (which, not surprisingly, did not work) and next to it a worn and faded book, full of numbers and figures that meant nothing to the little girl. In another there was the frame of an old metal bed, jammed hard up against the edge of the wall, the smallest bed she'd ever seen. And that was it. That was all there was to indicate that there had ever been any form of human habitation in the lighthouse. Except, that is, for the graffiti.

There was graffiti, everywhere. It was scrawled across the walls, in every room and even over those few pieces of furniture that remained. Most of the graffiti was incomprehensible, but she understood enough to know what had been written was obscene and viciously cruel. She tried to ignore it, and climbed further and further up, until finally she arrived at a room which appeared to be some sort of kitchen. It, too, was absolutely tiny, and covered in the same distressing graffiti. There was a little worktop on which sat an old rusted hob, with an assortment of kitchen utensils lying around, rusted too. Some cabinets clung to the walls, their doors hanging off or missing altogether. Thick mould covered every surface. The little girl looked in all the cabinets, hoping to perhaps find an old tin or two, but there was nothing.

She stepped back onto the stairs, and took a moment to decide what to do. She'd climbed higher than she realised – it wasn't far now to the top, the lantern light was just above her, but the stairs had worsened the higher she'd climbed. The last few steps looked incredibly worn, and quite precarious, but there was nothing else for it – she had to find out where she was, how else would she find her way home?

The stairs shook terribly, and for a second she thought she wouldn't make it. It was with tremendous relief therefore that she finally reached the top, but her relief was short lived - the floor of the lantern light was covered in thousands and thousands of tiny shards of glass! Even with decent shoes she wouldn't have dared stand on it. Instead, and as she had really no other option, she stepped outside, onto the balcony that ran right around the lantern light. In places the balcony was almost completely eroded, and the handrail too was very loose – she kept her back hard up against the lantern light, clinging where she could to its broken frame as she worked her away around. It was actually quite terrifying, but the little girl was once again made oblivious the danger, and too distracted to care - the view was simply amazing!

'I can see for miles' she said to herself, 'miles and miles and miles....'

Away in the one direction the sea disappeared to the horizon, shimmering so brightly in the sunlight that the little girl had to shade her eyes and eventually, to look away. In the other direction, rolling hills covered in forest stretched endlessly to the opposite horizon, all greens and golds, oranges and reds. It was stunning. Looking down (not that she really wanted to, but neither could she help herself!) way below, the base of the lighthouse was lost in the continual spray from the sea crashing against the rocks. It was hypnotic.

The little girl might have stayed there for hours, regardless of how scary it was, had she the proper clothes to protect her. But it was unbelievably cold, and the old raincoat was so badly torn that the freezing wind was blowing right through her. She knew that she had to get home. She couldn't stay another night, without food, and it was just too cold, even inside the lighthouse. (She'd seen a fireplace in the hall, and the remnants of a fire. Some of the other rooms also had disused fireplaces, but without matches, she had no way of lighting a fire.)

Returning her gaze back to the landward side of the lighthouse, she looked for some sign of the port, but there was nothing. She did vaguely recognise the direction from which she must have come through the forest the night before, so she took her bearings as best she could, and then made her way carefully back down the stairs to the door in the hall.

Taking one last look up into the stairwell, the little girl wrapped the smelly old raincoat around her, and stepped outside. Just as she pulled the door to, she was sure she heard something – something like a sigh? She wasn't sure – she looked up at the lighthouse towering above her, maybe she just imagined it?

Suddenly it all seemed very frightening - the empty lighthouse, covered in that the awful graffiti - and the little girl turned and ran away as fast as she could across the rocks! She didn't look back until she reached the edge of the forest – and there the old lighthouse sat, silently, on the promontory in the distance. The little girl wasn't sure what she expected, perhaps that the lighthouse might have chased after her, over the rocks and still be towering over her? It was ridiculous to think that, and as she continued to look at the lighthouse standing silhouetted against the bright blue sky, the little girl thought how marvellous it was, resting there, so tall and elegant. For a second the sun glinted from the lighthouse lantern, and it appeared to the little girl as if a fantastic light momentarily winked at her. It was only for a moment – 'I'm just being silly' she thought, and with one last look, headed back into the forest.

The little girl did her best to stick to her bearings, but again, became completely lost – the day wore on, and she could neither find her way back to the lighthouse, nor to the port. It started to rain, and despite the old raincoat, she was soon soaked through. She began to cough, her breathing coming harder and harder, until finally she could hardly catch a breath at all. Her legs gave way, and she fell, wheezing and crying onto the damp forest floor. In the distance she heard voices, and for a second imagined there were lights flickering in the gloom – was it the lighthouse, winking at her again? I'm just being silly she thought. She tried to call out but her voice was barely a whisper. The world began to dissolve, when suddenly a face was above hers, hands were lifting her up, a voice was calling: 'Here! Here! Over here!' She floated up through the air, trees swaying all around her, other voices shouting too – she kept trying to call out, but no one was listening, no one was listening – a voice in her ear asked 'What's that? What did you say?'

'The lighthouse saved me' she cried feebly, again, over and over. 'The lighthouse saved me'.

Her father and everyone else were overjoyed when the little girl was brought out from the forest. But she was desperately ill. A fever consumed her, and she lay for many days, hardly breathing at all. But gradually, her strength returned, and before long everyone in the port was delighted to see the little girl, up and about, and once again sitting with the old harbour master, laughing her infectious laugh at his ridiculous faces and tall tales.

It seemed to everyone that, apart from having a slight limp from when she fell on the rocks, the little girl was completely back to normal. But, as for the little girl herself...? Well, well, she felt very different indeed. She was overcome with such an intense fascination for the lighthouse, a fascination, an obsession in fact, that she could neither fully comprehend nor control. Put simply, she found that she just could not stop thinking about it. The lighthouse engulfed her every waking moment. Any fear that she'd felt was forgotten, replaced by this persistent obsession. All she wanted to do was to go back, and to find out everything she could about the lighthouse, about what had happened and why it was so ruined and unjustly neglected.

But for some reason, nobody wanted to talk about it. Whenever she mentioned the lighthouse, to anyone, she was met with either curt and sometimes angry replies, or sometimes no reply at all. No-one was prepared to discuss it with her, not even old Ben. If she asked him, he would just laugh, and change the subject. He never brought the lighthouse up, and only once spoke to her about the night she had spent there.

'So you've 'ad a wee adventure to yerself, 'ave you, li'l miss?' he said, one day not long after she'd recovered. 'Well, ah hope you got that outta' yer system – now you best stay away from there, mind. Not safe up there – you stay away. Wouldn't want you getting hurt now.'

She knew, or at least she told herself she knew, that he was just being kind and looking out for her, but his subtle admonishment, and indeed everyone else's conspiratorial silence, only fuelled her curiosity further.

Of course she asked her father, but he didn't really want to talk about it either, well at least not that specific lighthouse. He thought that if Ben had told her to stay away, then: stay away. It really wasn't any of their business. He was happy enough to talk to her about lighthouses in general though, and he even appeared to delight in explaining to her how they actually worked. She sat and listened intently as he described authoratively, in that all too academic tone of his, how lighthouses were really very simple things: that inside the lantern light, there was a lamp and a prism, and how the lamp when lit, its light would be magnified by the prism, and that was how the fantastic beams of light were created. She was absolutely enthralled by his descriptions, and he found books for her, full of wonderful diagrams that explained everything in incredible detail. She poured over them, staring endlessly at the wonderful drawings and photographs and paintings. There were so many of them, so many different types of lighthouses, all shapes and sizes. She'd had no idea. And they were all so beautiful, although of course none so beautiful as her lighthouse (as she had come to think of it!)

She wondered too at the character of the lighthouse keeper, the person who would stay for days, months even, all alone in the lighthouse. She envied such a person tremendously. How wonderful, she thought, it would be to live in a lighthouse!

It was such a joy for the little girl, to fill her days, discovering all these new and incredible things. But her nights were quite the opposite: she was plagued by dreams that were darkly troubling and despondent, dreams in which the lighthouse was torn down and ravaged, sometimes by the stormy sea, sometimes by a black, shapeless monster, an awful shadow which would rise up out of the forest and shatter the lighthouse with a single stroke of one of its numerous tortured and crooked limbs. Sometimes, and worst of all, the lighthouse was destroyed by hordes of ghostly figures, whose ugly faces would be lit up in flickering torchlight, distorted and enraged. They'd be shouting dreadful things, repeating those dreadful words of the graffiti, the words creeping from their hideously misshapen grimacing mouths, spewing such spiteful condemnation and hatred. Like ants over a carcass, they would swarm over the lighthouse, devouring it, and leaving it little more than a ruin, which they would then set alight, laughing insanely as the lighthouse was consumed in the agonising flames.

These nightmares upset the little girl terribly. She so wanted to tell someone about them, to find some solace from the ominous sense of dread she sometimes felt, and indeed, maybe even some comfort too, from the obsessive longing for the lighthouse? But she couldn't. She couldn't speak about it, even to her father, who, though she loved dearly, had never been one to invite such intimacy. The only person she felt she could completely confide in was the old harbour master's wife.

One quiet evening, she poured her heart out to the old woman, how wonderful she thought the lighthouse was, how magnificent it was, and of her utter bewilderment – why, why did no one else seem to care? She was so confused. The little girl talked and talked, as the harbour master's wife sat, quietly listening, nodding occasionally and all the while knitting away in front of the flickering fire that crackled in the hearth of her small dark cottage.

'You don't worry yourself' she said kindly, when the little girl finally stopped, almost breathless from her unbridled confession. 'That ol' man of mine isn't as tough as he seems. You ask 'im again in the morning.'

So the next day, emboldened by her conversation with the harbour master's wife, the little girl asked Ben, as they sat down on the quayside, quite directly, and before her resolve failed her:

'Please tell me, Ben – please tell me about the lighthouse.'

'Now, li'l miss, y'know– '

'Oh, please tell me' she pleaded, interrupting him. 'Please, please, please, please....'

The old harbour master, at last, it seemed, could not resist her cheerful persistence or her stubborn gaze any longer.

'Alright' he laughed, 'alright. But you tell no-one I told ya', y'hear? Promise.'

'I promise' the little girl said, solemnly putting her hand on her heart.

The old harbour master cleared his throat, and in his thick local accent, began: 'It were ten years ago, almost to the day. Ten years - ah, you should'a seen this place back then. Never been such a port, I can tell ya'. Oh, it never stopped here, mind, never stopped, day and night. Sights and sounds you wouldn't believe! Every type of vessel you could ever imagine came into this port y'know, and ah seen every one of them. Betcha' ah have - seen every type of vessel fit to sail the seas at one time or another, right in this 'ere port, and ah berthed every one o' 'em too! T'was something to behold. Y'know, you could walk from one side of this here harbour to the other, sometimes, one boat to another, and never once see the sea below ya'. Not once.

Came from everywhere, from all over they did – all round the whole world. Trading ships mostly, they were the best, y'know, bringing such things, things you wouldn't believe – jewels and clothes and foods, fruits and such. You shoulda' seen all 'em shopkeepers and market traders back then, fighting over each other, trying to get the best deals, you should've seen 'em! Not a chance with 'em shipmates! Not a chance.

And the whalers – my, they were a tough lot. More scar than skin, I can tell you. Fearsome bunch, fearsome - did most of their talking with their fists! Some of the frigate sailors would take 'em on, never beat 'em mind, oh but what fights! Blood'n'teeth everywhere! They'd drink all day – see that one tavern we 'ave? They'rd be tavern after tavern reelin' with 'em, fightin' over the local girls, and they loved it they did, though they'd feign to swoon as the sight of 'em batterin' hell outta each other!

Oh, oh, ...and the fish – my oh my – everything you can imagine, haddock, carp, sea bass, monkfish, shellfish. Couldn't move for fish. Fearsome lookin' things some oh them, creatures from another world, feign to say a God could ever have made 'em. And this place didn't half reek of 'em either. A blind man could find this place from a thousand miles

I used to say – stink it did! But it was good times. Yeh, them's were good times, good times indeed.'

The old harbour master fell silent as he reminisced. The little girl nudged him.

'The lighthouse?'

'Yeh, the lighthouse – see, without the lighthouse .... well, let's see. That lighthouse was always 'ere, even when ah was a boy, for as long as ah can remember, it'd been 'ere. Never knew what came first, port or lighthouse. Don't matter much – all that matters is, you can't have one without t'other, see? See, we get storms here, sometimes, see, that's why. Ain't no use having a harbour if the boats can't get to it, eh? Especially in a storm, y'know? An' you don't want some capn' turnin' his boat around coz he ain't got no light to guide 'im in. No sir. Gotta' be good'n'clear. Well that lighthouse, that was a fine lighthouse. Fine as any ah've ever seen. And she had some light on 'er. Had a light brighter than the sun it was. Nevah' seen anything like it. Beams that seemed to almost reach out and touch you, y'know? Beams of light, you'd think went all the way to the horizon, all round the world! And she never failed us neither, not once, not ever.'

He paused, dropping his gaze, downcast to the harbour floor. When he continued, his voice had lost all its humour, and was all of a sudden, stern.

'Then, that night, that night- ten years ago it was, the worst storm we ever had around these parts. Waves high as mountains, ah'm telling ya'! And the wind – all the sinners in hell couldn't holler any louder, ah'm tellin' ya' true coz' ah seen it, with me own eyes. You'd think the flood was comin'! And there, in the middle of it all - a tanker. They're no small thing,

I can tell, them tankers, them's huge things, and this one was getting tossed about like it was a...like it was a stick – who'd 'ave been a sailor on that sad ship, I'm askin' ya'. Not me.'

The old harbour master looked up earnestly at the little girl. 'But no one was worried see, not really. Why would we? – lighthouse would see 'em alright. Worst storm in the world, didn't matter none – keep starboard of the light, and Bob's yer uncle, no problem. So we waited and waited, and waited – and nothin'. Just when it was needed most. Nothing. Not a thing. No light, nothin'.

The harbour master paused, before continuing in a voice that had become almost lifeless.

'Tanker sank, you know. We all seen it - thrown against the rocks, over and over. Lost all hands. Terrible.'

He paused again, sitting for a moment, silently staring out over the harbour towards the open sea.

'Well, nothing was the same after that, t'was beginning of the end. Trading ships still came for a while, but word got out. This port, not safe.' He shook his head sadly. 'It was the death knell. Shipping just stayed away. Who's gonna' come here? If I were a cap'n, I wouldn't. So everything just dried up. Shops all closed, folks moved away – no work, y' see. No money. Nothin'.'

He looked up, abruptly - 'all on account'a that damn lighthouse!' he said, sharply, and with a sudden flash of anger that shocked the little girl. She sat upright and completely still, looking with wide eyes as Ben's head sank down again. They sat like that for a while, saying nothing, in silence except for the sound of seawater gently lapping up against the harbour wall, and the screeching of some gulls hovering distantly overhead.

The little girl eventually broke their silence. 'But wasn't there a light-house keeper?' she prompted gently.

'Yeh, yeh' said the old harbour master. He roused himself. 'Yeh – him. No one ever saw him again. No surprise. Useless old drunk.'

'Did he...did he smash it all up?'

Ben looked at her, all of a sudden cautious. 'What do you mean?'

The little girl was suddenly a bit frightened of old Ben – he was staring at her, straight at her, deep into her eyes, his own eyes hard and unblinking.

'Well...it's just that, it's all messed up. You know, all the windows broken and everything', she said nervously. She wanted to ask him about the graffiti, but she couldn't. She would have been embarrassed to do so at the best of times, and Ben's stare unnerved her terribly. It was so unlike him.

'No, I don't know' he replied, quite harshly. 'Now you listen to me li'l miss. I told ya' before - nothing good can come from that place. Nothin'. You stay away. You just put it outta' yer mind.'

The little girl tried to do as Ben asked of her, but she couldn't. It all just seemed so wrong. The storm, the wrecked tanker, it wasn't the lighthouse's fault, it couldn't have been. And anyway, it was of no matter. If they wanted their port back, the lighthouse would need to be restored, and that was all there was to it. She could see this if no-one else could. So she decided that something had to be done.

She began a petition to have the lighthouse saved, but no-one signed it. She tried to raise money from donations, but no-one gave her even a single penny. She tried to enlist some of the trades-people, those that there were, the mason and electrician and carpenter – but none of them was prepared to help her, not even for one minute's worth of effort. Even Ben wouldn't help – and he, like everyone else in the town, began to actively shun the little girl. No-one would talk to her any more. Ben wouldn't even sit with her on the quayside any longer. It made the little girl dreadfully upset, more so because she couldn't understand what she was doing that was so wrong. She was just trying to help.

Overcome with frustration and loneliness, she'd cry herself to sleep almost every night. But, come the next day, she'd find the strength of will, somehow, despite the cold stares and silent reproach, to carry on. She pestered everyone she could, exhausted every opportunity.

Eventually, the little girl had had enough.

'If they won't help me,' she said to herself, stubbornly, 'then I'll do it myself!'

Of course there was one problem – she had no idea how to get there! No-one would tell her even that. She could try to get there by herself, but she was scared and obviously quite justifiably certain that she would get lost. So she went again to the harbour master's wife, who listened patiently once more as the little girl poured out her considerable frustration. All she wanted to do was save the lighthouse – why was that so wrong? And what was wrong with everyone, that they wouldn't even tell her how to get there? The harbour master's wife suggested, with a little twinkle in her eye, that perhaps what the girl needed was a nice, long, refreshing walk, perhaps along the old cliff-side path, to clear her head. Maybe that would do the trick. It was all that the little girl needed to hear.

The very next day, she packed a bag with all the tools she could scrounge, some dusters, a brush and pan. She made up a small lunch and took the long walk out of the port that led up to the steep path along the cliff edge.

The sun was high in the cloudless sky when the lighthouse eventually came into view. It was already past lunchtime, and the little girl was hungry, tired, and her knee was aching dreadfully. But at the sight of the lighthouse all her worries evaporated. She felt such an exhilaration, spurring her on, and she reached the lighthouse, breathless but happy shortly after.

Standing at the bottom of the stone steps that led to the lighthouse door, she stared up at the lighthouse towering over her. It was so strange to be back, and memories of huddling freezing cold in the doorway came back to her, giving her pause. She had to admit, she did feel some small degree of trepidation as she climbed the steps and pushed open the lighthouse door.

But once inside she felt these worries too evaporate, as she looked up again into the wonderful spiral of the stair rising above her. She could have stared and stared, but ever practical, the little girl reminded herself that she was here for a reason, and it was already late. 'Time to get this place sorted' she said to herself.

It was difficult to know where to start – there was so much needing done. But she didn't let that put her off. 'First, tidy' she thought. She started at the top, sweeping up all the leaves, and dusting down every surface she could reach. It took her the remainder of the day to do just that, but by the time she was finished, the lighthouse was already beginning to look much better!

She stood in the hall, tired and dirty, and stared up again at the stairwell. The late afternoon sunlight was streaming through the little windows, all the dust that she'd disturbed by her hard day's work was lit up like golden glitter, creating beams of dancing light, a whole latticework of them, interspersed through the stairs themselves. 'It's so beautiful' she thought dreamily to herself. 'So beautiful'.

She could have stayed there forever, but she knew it was getting towards evening, and she had a long way to go to get home. Pulling on the old raincoat, she gathered up her things, and was about to leave when a voice from somewhere above her, whispered:

'Thank you.'

The little girl looked around, startled. It was the same voice; she recognised it for sure, even if, this time, it wasn't shouting at her.

'Thank you' the voice said again, clearly and quite distinctly. The little girl looked around, but she couldn't see anyone, she couldn't even be sure where the voice was coming from – it seemed to come from everywhere and yet nowhere. It was a deep, deep voice, gentle though unmistakably aged.

'I'm sorry for shouting at you before' it continued. 'I thought you might have been like...... the others.'

The little girl had no idea who the others were, but she was pretty certain she was not one of them, and she said so.

'So I see' the voice replied, and, as if sensing the little girl's apprehension, continued: 'You don't need to be afraid. I won't hurt you. I simply wanted to thank you for what you've done. It has been some time since anyone has shown me such kindness.'

'It was my pleasure' she said, politely. 'Are you the lighthouse keeper?'

'No, no. There's no lighthouse keeper here.'

The voice didn't elucidate any further, but somehow, it didn't matter. The answer came as no surprise to the little girl - she knew instinctively that it wasn't any actual person that was talking to her. It was the lighthouse itself, and why not - she was still perfectly young and innocent enough to accept the fact entirely and without question.

The lighthouse had gone completely silent, and she was suddenly at a loss – she so wanted to keep talking, but the sun was beginning to set.

'I have to go' she shouted up the stairwell. 'I'll be back tomorrow.' She waited, but the lighthouse said nothing further.

All the way down the cliff-side path she kept stopping to look back over her shoulder, hoping for something – she didn't know what. The lighthouse finally disappeared from view, and she ran the rest of the way home, her thoughts racing too. The lighthouse had spoken to her, it had spoken to her – she couldn't believe it! All that night she tossed and turned, so excited was she by what had happened, and yet worried too – in the darkness doubts began to confound her: had the lighthouse really spoken to her? Had she just imagined it?

The morning couldn't come quickly enough. She was up and dressed long before her father rose. She packed herself a bag again with a small lunch and more cleaning stuff, and rushed out, reaching the cliffs even before the sun had appeared above the sea's horizon. She ran most of the way, overjoyed when the lighthouse came once again into view. She almost threw herself through its door.

'Hello?' she called, breathlessly up into the stairwell. 'Hello?!'

The kind old voice replied almost immediately, with a sombre yet comforting: 'Good morning.'

'Oh – eh, good morning' the little girl replied, properly.

'Isn't it a beautiful day?' the lighthouse said.

'Yes, oh yes, it's beautiful!' enthused the little girl in exaggerated accord. 'It's just beautiful!'

'I didn't think you'd still be here' she added, once she'd caught her breath.

'I'm always here' said the lighthouse, quite matter of factly, although tinged with a subtle sadness that was lost on the little girl.

'Oh – that's wonderful' she said, beaming ecstatically. 'Wonderful.'

'I am pleased that you think so' said the lighthouse. If it could, the lighthouse would have smiled too. As it was, the little girl smiled enough for both of them – she was in heaven! She tried to contain herself though, not only out of a sense of decorum, but also, she had to admit, to quell her nervous embarrassment. Her cheeks were burning!

She turned around, to hang up the old raincoat, and said the first thing that came into her head: 'This place is such a mess'. She immediately regretted it.

'Oh, I'm sorry – I didn't mean -'

'That's ok' said the lighthouse. 'You are right. Though, today, not quite as much of a mess as it was yesterday?'

The little girl knew that the lighthouse was referring to what she'd done the day before, and she felt her cheeks burn even more.

'I just tidied up a little' she said humbly, flattered and blushing uncontrollably.

'Well, it was most appreciated.'

'Oh, but I'm not finished' she countered. 'I've brought more things today.' She opened her bag and held it up. 'See?' she said.

'There is no need, really' the lighthouse said after a slight pause.

'Oh but I want to. I want to – you shouldn't have been left in such a state. It's not right.'

'No, perhaps-'

'And whoever did this, they should be ashamed of themselves' the little girl interrupted. In her mind, she visualised the terrible faces from her dreams, whoever they were, perhaps 'the others' that the lighthouse had referred to. 'It's horrible, horrible what they did.'

'You...you need not be so harsh on them – I'm sure they believed I deserved it.'

'No-one deserves to be treated this way' the little girl said, angrily and with a maturity beyond her tender years. She added stubbornly: 'I am going to make this right. I am. I'm going to fix you up, you just watch me!'

And the little girl was true to her word. That day, and every day after, she came, working longer and longer hours, happily talking away all the time to the lighthouse as she did so.

There were many things that she just could not do as properly as she wished: fixing the broken windows was beyond her, as was the door - she couldn't hammer nails as well as she would like, nor could she replace screws properly. She just wasn't strong enough. But she was inventive, and evidently resourceful. She covered all the windows in sticky tape, tons of it. She filled gaps in the door with cloth and taped that up too. She scraped down all the flaking paint that she could reach on the outside of the lighthouse, did the same on the inside, and then actually painted it! Brushes she 'borrowed' from her father, and from old Ben's tool store. The paint she bought herself, from her own savings. As some parts of the lighthouse were quite inaccessible, she tied paint brushes to a broom handle in order to reach further, often stretching precariously over the stairs to do so.

The stairs themselves were a constant worry. She tied rope around them, attaching them to anything she could in an effort to strengthen them, but they were pretty damaged, well beyond repair really. The best she could do was clean them, and this she did with a toothbrush, taking an age to get out all the grime and dirt that had accumulated in the fine carved detail.

She scrubbed down every surface, cleaned and polished everything. When she had finished painting and cleaning, she then began to add some decorative touches of her own. She fashioned curtains out of table cloths, which she hung in all the windows. She put flowers in all the windows too, in the fireplace grate, and on the table next to the old logbook. The logbook itself she dried, by patiently opening it page by page and leaving it to lie in the afternoon sunlight.

It troubled her terribly though, the graffiti, which in places she could neither completely erase nor reach to paint over. She apologised profusely to the lighthouse, about this and all the other perceived deficiencies on her part that prevented her from properly rectifying everything. The lighthouse, if asked, would have had to admit it was confused, initially, that the little girl should be *so* self-critical. It re-assured her constantly, without any expectation necessarily that its words would have any impact - it realised that this was simply her nature, a nature so infinitely kind hearted and caring that the lighthouse, and indeed anyone, had they seen the efforts she made, might have had some considerable trouble accepting. As the days passed, the lighthouse constantly marvelled at the little girl's capacity for empathy, which extended not just to it, but also to others not necessarily deserving of such attention and consideration. Often she would leave to fulfil some task on behalf of someone else, to buy stamps or deliver something, or to tend to some other menial chore back in the port. She did these things selflessly and with equanimity, and the lighthouse in turn learnt to praise the little girl perpetually in everything she did, regardless.

On the little girl's part, although she could not put it into words, she discovered a solace that she had never known: the lighthouse listened. No-one, she realised, no-one had ever really listened to her before. She could tell the lighthouse absolutely anything, all her secrets, her hopes, her dreams, her worries, her most trivial and ridiculous thought or concern. Occasionally the lighthouse would offer some comment, and she in turn loved listening to its wise observations. She often could not fully understand what the lighthouse meant, but it was enough that the lighthouse took the time to do so, was never condescending and always spoke to her with care and genuine concern.

The only thing that they never discussed, and the little girl never even dared mention it, was the night the tanker sank

– she wanted to, but something made her stop. Somehow, as if by silent, mutual consent, it was forbidden.

Eventually, after several weeks of hard work, everything that the little girl could fix, was fixed. All that remained was the lantern light. She stood atop of the stairs, looking down at the thousands and thousands and thousands of pieces of glass, glittering in the sunlight. There appeared not to be a single clue as to how this multitude of pieces might fit together, nor indeed which pieces came from the lantern light and which came from the prism. And she had no idea even how the prism might have looked. 'How am I going to fix *this*?' she thought to herself, the enormity of the task momentarily confounding her.

'Leave it' the lighthouse said, quietly, seeming to read her thoughts, as it had so often done before.

'But-'

'It's ok, really. You have done enough. More than enough.'

'But your light…?'

'Leave it. You can't fix it.'

'I could try……'

Her words hung in the air. The lighthouse said nothing. Its unusual silence confused the little girl, making her feel awkward and suddenly rather self conscious. She bent down and picked up one of the tiny shards of glass that covered the lantern light floor. Holding it up to her eye, she turned it slowly between her fingertips. A rainbow of pale colours, greens and blues and aquamarine, danced within. It was so beautiful, so, *so* beautiful. How could something as beautiful as this have become so…..abused? She had to know. She just had to.

'Ben told me-', she began, tentatively.

'Ben?' the lighthouse interrupted her.

'Yes, Ben – the harbour master?'

'Ah, Ben, is that his name? And what did Ben tell you?'

'He told me - he told me your light didn't come on. That night – the night of the storm?'

It was a second or two before the lighthouse answered.

'Did he tell you why?'

'No, no – he just said that they waited and waited, for your light to come on, and it didn't. Something about the lighthouse keeper – he was drunk? And then the tanker sank...'

Again the lighthouse paused. 'Yes' was all it said, tonelessly.

The lighthouse went very quiet, and the little girl sat, nervous, afraid she'd made the lighthouse angry. But her reticence was immediately overcome by her curiosity. She persevered.

'Ben said it was so unexpected. They'd never worried before, your light always came on he said.'

Again, a pause.

'There was a time......' the lighthouse said, eventually, and its words, like the little girl's beforehand, hung momentarily in the air. In a voice hollow and unmistakably bleak, the lighthouse added: 'It *was* all my fault. They're not wrong.'

'But it wasn't your fault' the little girl insisted. 'It was the keeper – if he was drunk? Surely?'

'You don't understand' said the lighthouse. 'My keeper was certainly drunk. He was always drunk, he always had been. It wasn't his fault – it was nobody's fault, but mine.'

The little girl couldn't help but feel some anger rise in her, anger at the lighthouse for reasons she couldn't explain. The lighthouse was right – she didn't understand.

'Well – why didn't you put your light on? Was it because your light was smashed?'

'No, my light was not smashed.'

'Well, why then, why didn't you? Why?' The little girl could feel tears welling up in her eyes. The lighthouse fell silent once again. She stared hard around her. 'Why?' she said again, quietly but insistently. She waited and waited, but the lighthouse sat silent and said nothing at all.

Finally she stood up – the sun had almost set on the horizon, its last golden rays of light streaking across the sea to where she stood. She looked down at the shard of glass still gripped gently in her fingers. A single tear trickled down her cheek as she laid the shard delicately back onto the floor of the lantern light. More tears followed, silently falling, and she turned and began to climb back down the stairs.

The lighthouse voice stopped her.

'It wasn't that I didn't' it said '– I couldn't.'

The little girl looked up, and she could only stand and listen, with an increasing sadness, as the lighthouse continued, in a voice at once almost interminably weary and yet dispassionately resolute: 'There was a time - it seems so long ago now, I can hardly even recall – my light, my light was simply a part of me. It could never have occurred to me then that there was any other way for me to be. I expect that others understood and accepted this likewise to be the case. Certainly no-one ever had any call to question it. Some, I don't doubt, might have wondered at my place, if not my purpose, in the world – we are isolated, by necessity. But I had no sense of this. If you had asked me back then, if you had even used the term, I would not have understood what you meant. I was what I was and I did what I did, as surely and confidently as anyone might do so when they fulfil completely their purpose. And I did so, I might add, with aplomb.' The little girl remembered old Ben's comments, visualising in her mind what tremendous beams of light might have at one time emanated from the lighthouse, beams of light stretching to the endless horizon he'd said...

'But at some point, I do not recall exactly when, I began to notice that my light was becoming ......weaker. Every time it was needed, it was slightly less powerful than before, just not quite as strong, not quite as sure? As time went on, admittedly only a relatively short space of time, the worse it became. Not so much that anyone would notice you understand, and never to the point that my light could not be effective, or at least so I thought. But, then, one day, my light went out, altogether.'

The lighthouse paused, and in the silence the little girl imagined that she could actually feel the empty distress that the memory had provoked. Her heart pounded in her chest.

'I told no-one' the lighthouse continued, whispering again: 'I told no-one.'

'But there must have been someone?' the little girl wanted to interject, but before she could do so the lighthouse carried on, its voice still uncommonly weary and sombre: 'You have asked me 'why?'' it said. 'Why I did not put on my light? Had it been possible to do so, do you not think I would have? But I could not. I could not.

If you were to ask me why, why not, I cannot answer you. I wish that I could, I wish I knew. To be unable to answer you is such a source of dissatisfaction to me – it has been my considerable pleasure to listen to you as you have talked, and whenever you have asked of me a question, raised any query or expressed any lack of understanding, on any matter, I have endeavoured always to try to answer you, as truthfully as I can, in an effort to assuage your concerns, salve your curiosity, or solve your problem. But as I say, if you were to ask of me why my light does not work – I do not know why. It is a question I have obviously asked myself, repeatedly, and have found the question to be wanting, endless, and in itself the asking of it, debilitating.

Of the causes responsible that I have considered, there are potentially many – I am certainly old as you may have noticed, though not so old that one might think it credible, but it is only to this condition that I can ascribe any sensible rationale. For I have also wondered at and entertained fanciful and truly ridiculous notions. I could ascribe it to being a form of punishment perhaps, a punishment inflicted upon me, by some unseen and vindictive power. But for what reason - my arrogance? My vanity? Perhaps it is a punishment borne of a jealous evil, in spite for my good fortune? Perhaps.

Or perhaps I might ascribe it to some technical flaw, some inherent deficiency in my physical condition? Or perhaps I'm cursed? Or perhaps, perhaps it is simply my destiny. Perhaps it is everyone's – that we are all destined to lose our faculties, to succumb and to fail. If so, if this is the inevitable consequence of existence, then so be it. I could then carry that burden with some small measure of consolation. But regardless, I cannot help but be consumed by a sense of injustice, that this consequence was inflicted upon me in such an incomprehensible way, indiscriminately and without any valid reason that I can comprehend, or accept.

I should rage at it, this injustice, I should, but I have found no recourse to appeal. Even that is denied me. How could I? I am more than alone here, nor even abandoned – I am .... dispossessed.'

Much of what the lighthouse said the little girl could not really understand. There were words that meant nothing to her, phrases and terminology that were beyond her. But she could feel deep within an awakened empathy for the lighthouse – its profound sadness and sense of loss a reflection of her own, and until that moment, unrealised, loneliness.

'Was there no-one you could tell?' she asked.

The lighthouse fell silent yet again, as the sun finally set beyond the far horizon. A darkness descended upon them both, and with it, a cold breeze spiralled gently up and through the lighthouse, the lighthouse's words seeming to float lifelessly upon it: 'How could I admit to being what I had become, to being what I *am*, when what I am is not enough? What use would I be? What use, *is* a lighthouse, without a light?'

How much time passed the little girl had no idea. Time, in fact, seemed to stop. The darkness deepened unnaturally, and with it the cold intensified, wrapping itself around the little girl like a frozen coat and chilling her, both inside and out. It was everything she could do to stop her teeth from chattering. She wrapped her arms as tightly as she could around herself, trying but failing to keep warm.

'You should go' the lighthouse said.

'I don't want to.' She knew that the lighthouse meant go, go and don't come back.

'Go' it insisted.

'But I could-'

'No'. The lighthouse was emphatic. 'No. You have done enough.'

'I could explain – they'll understand. They'll remember. They'll remember how......wonderful you were.'

'Wonderful? Perhaps, and perhaps they might. But for why? At best, their forgiveness – but even if it were proffered, would it matter? They died. They all died, that night, that night of the storm. All those poor souls, and I did not save them. Go.'

The little girl went home that night, and cried and cried and cried, and could not stop crying. Her father tried to console her, but to no avail. He could not understand what was wrong; she knew he never would, even if she had the means to explain it. She hardly understood herself.

Finally she fell into a fitful sleep, fraught with dreams of her beautiful lighthouse being destroyed by huge waves crashing down upon it, as she lay curled up, one instant upon its stone steps, the next upon its stone floor, and all the time scratching her fingernails upon the lighthouse door, begging to be let in, begging to be let out.

For many days afterwards the little girl did not leave her room. When she did eventually venture back out into the port, no-one could help but notice what a change had befallen her. Her pallor, already colourless and sallow, was replaced by a deathly greyness that made her father fear once more for her health. Similarly, her familiar enthusiasm for all things had evaporated: she talked to no-one, and no-one dared to talk to her. Only her eyes retained some remnant of her intensity for life, and at times took on a furious aspect. But otherwise she moved through the port like a ghost, haunting the place to the point that the port's inhabitants began avoiding her as if she carried some terrible and contagious disease.

It was not lost upon old Ben, who would talk to his wife about the little girl, secretly, in the confines of their small cottage. 'You should speak to her' his wife would suggest, knowing that it would fall upon deaf ears. He would shake his head and mutter 'Not for me to meddle in the lives of others. Not for me.' Eventually the harbour master's wife took it upon herself to do so.

She called unexpectedly one day at the doctor's surgery, and with the pretence of needing assistance with some fictitious chore, she inquired of the doctor if she might ask it of his little girl.

'She's not herself' he replied soberly, with a feeble resistance that almost immediately was conceded: 'By all means you may ask.'

The harbour master's wife did not spend long with the little girl. She was lying in her bed facing the wall, and said nothing to the harbour master's wife when she came in. Settling herself on the end of the bed, the harbour masters wife patted the little girl gently, slowly and kindly stroking the hair on the back of her head. 'You have to be what you'll be' she said. She laid a small torch and a pair of knitted fingerless gloves on the bedside cabinet. 'You'll need these' she added, and then left.

The little girl sat up as her bedroom door closed. She picked up the gloves, and then the torch, flicking it, on and off, on and off, on and off. For the first time in many, many weeks, she smiled.

The lighthouse door was unusually difficult to open. The little girl pushed and pushed, until it eventually creaked open far enough for her to squeeze through. She said nothing as she climbed the stairs, and only when she reached the top did she dare even touch the walls of the lighthouse (she had always done so in the past, always felt the need to steady herself as she had climbed the stairs beforehand – but not today. Somehow the stairs no longer troubled her.) She ran her fingers over the concave surface. 'Hello' she said, still smiling. She had no expectation of a response and she got none, but it did not bother her. She had work to do.

The first thing was to separate out those shards of glass that belonged to the lantern light and those that belonged to the prism. Thankfully, on a closer inspection, there was a slight difference between the two – the glass for the lantern light was thinner, lighter, the pieces smaller and more regular. The prism glass was much harder, its pieces much more randomly sized and shaped.

She gathered up *all* the shards of glass and brought them down into the lighthouse. Once she'd separated the pieces, lantern light and prism (this took her some weeks!) she carried the prism pieces back up to the lantern light – this she would fix last. She needed to fix the lantern light itself first. It was freezing working up there – the summer months had long since passed. It was now autumn, with winter looming, and she knew that fixing the prism was going to take her a very long time. She'd need the glass back in place in the lantern light to give her protection from the wind at least.

It was some task however. There were eight sides to the lantern light, eight sides all exactly the same, and no way of knowing which pieces came from which sides. Even to know which piece fitted with which, she had to look for the tiniest of clues, a small scratch here, a minute crack there – it was truly the most ridiculous of jigsaws – pieces, thousands of them, all indeterminate, and no picture to follow! Only some small number of shards still stuck in the lantern light frame gave her any indication of where to start.

She examined every piece - the inside of the lighthouse was literally covered in the glass shards! They were laid out everywhere, on every step of the stairs, in every one of the lighthouses tiny rooms, on every surface. When the autumn sun on occasion burst through the little windows, it lit up the lighthouse like the inside of a massive diamond, with such a sparkling intensity that the little girl at times had to shield her eyes, so gloriously bright was it.

Once she'd determined which pieces belonged to which side she had to fashion a way of attaching them to each other, and in turn attaching them back into the lantern light frame. Her trusty tape was the solution. She formed long thin strips of tape, layered together for strength, and then fixed the pieces to the sticky side. She then wrapped the strips, one by one, from the bottom up around the outside of the lantern light. It really was beyond precarious, definitely perilous work, especially when she had to stretch to the topmost part of the frame. The balcony was as unsteady as it had always been, the wind howled constantly at such a height, and was often accompanied by freezing, driving rain. Sometimes the little girl imagined that some invisible god must have been enraged by her efforts, and was throwing its fury against her. But she drew the old raincoat ever tighter around herself, pulled its hood down low over her head, and persisted.

Eventually it was complete. All the lantern light pieces were back in place. There were inevitably a number of gaps, several, in fact, but she wrapped more and more tape around the inside until the whole lantern light was sealed. It was with some satisfaction that she sat back and looked at what she had accomplished. For the first time she stood inside the lantern light, without the terrible buffeting of the wind, and looked out through the, admittedly, somewhat blurred windows that she had created - the view was still awe inspiring! She could hardly imagine a place more stunning.

By the time the lantern light was finished, autumn was well and truly over. Winter was settling in, the weather was turning harsh, and the light faded earlier day by day. She began work on the prism immediately, but this proved to be much more difficult. It was by necessity delicate work, every piece she had to examine again in exacting detail, turning them between her fingertips, and often in the gloom of evening, lit only by the pale light from the small torch the harbour master's wife had given her. Sitting up in the lantern light, for hours on end, it was inevitable that she also became very cold. Her leg ached terribly, to the point that she developed a constant limp, and her hands would lose all their feeling, despite the gloves which the harbour master's wife had knitted for her. It was perhaps a blessing. Where the glass in the lantern light had been small, the larger pieces of the prism glass were much more irregular, and much sharper. Her fingertips were cut to shreds. Every night when she got home she had to clean the numerous cuts, soaking her fingers in disinfected water which made them sting terribly as the feeling returned. Every morning she wrapped her fingers in plasters, which in turn would be completely shredded again and covered in blood by the end of the day.

She tried to hide her hands from her father, but it was impossible, and neither could she tell him where she was going, or what she was doing. So she lied, and told him that she was spending all her time with the harbour master's wife, and that the harbour master's wife was teaching her to knit and sew. She wasn't sure that he entirely believed her, but he didn't pursue it with her. He was simply relieved, and appeared content that his daughter was well again, and anyway, he was always so busy at the surgery that they rarely talked, about anything other than daily necessities.

And so it went on, month after month. The little girl still had chores to do, and occasionally she did visit the harbour masters wife, to sit quietly with her in the warmth of her small cottage. But otherwise she spent every minute at the lighthouse, her whole attention focussed on her Herculean task.

One could be forgiven for thinking that the little girl might have despaired at times – the task she had set herself was truly unimaginable, and the conditions desperately remote and inhospitable. But she didn't. It was hard, slow painful and frustrating work, but some strange aura seemed to protect and comfort her. Once before she had encountered such a unique sense of comfort in the lighthouse, but this was different. She talked as she had talked before, but, in those interminable hours as she sat on the cold steel floor of the lantern light, she talked of things undiscovered, revealing uncharted depths of emotions and feelings that she'd felt but never before realised. The only sound the little girl heard in return was the echo of her own sweet voice, perpetually repeating her words back to her, as if conferring upon her some universal acceptance and forgiveness of her intimate confessions.

And if she had been asked, what sustained her in those long dark days, she could not have answered - there were no words for that. At best all she would have been able to say was that she was content, content and......happy. And that she never once felt alone, despite the fact that the lighthouse said nothing to her.

At last, late one evening, the prism was complete. Like the lantern light, there were gaps, many of them, but it was on the whole as intact and to the best of the little girl's abilities, exact to its original form as it could be, even if it were a little lopsided and not as entirely symmetrical as she had hoped. Regardless, completed, it still stood as tall as the little girl, like an enormous jewel, almost filling the whole of the lantern light room. She inserted the very last shard, stood back as far as she could, and allowed herself a moment to admire her accomplishment, as she had done with the lantern light before. It was however beyond her comprehension how beautiful the prism was – she could never have pictured it so, despite it having literally taken shape right in front of her, gradually by her own hands. Tears suddenly filled her eyes, but she wiped them away. There was one last thing she had to do.

Kneeling down, she took the small torch and inserted it into what she assumed had been the lamp-holder that sat at the base of the prism. Her hands trembled almost uncontrollably, and for a second she couldn't find the torch switch. Once located, she hesitated only for a moment, before turning it on.

At first it seemed that nothing happened. Her heart sank. She had hoped, so desperately hoped, to see those magnificent beams of light, but there was nothing. Only a slight and shallow glow filled the prism, a pale and insipid light that was as far removed as possible from what she had imagined. But as she looked closer into the prism, as she looked deep within she saw something remarkable – tiny, tiny beams of light, thousands of them, hundreds of thousands and thousands of them, blues, greens, and aquamarine, were bouncing this way and that, everywhere. It was mesmerising. She put her hand out to touch the prism, and for the first time ever, she felt warmth emanate from a part of the lighthouse. Her scarred fingertips tingled at it.

With the sensation came, as always, the pressing need to return home. She wondered for a moment whether she might leave the torch. It was so dark, and she'd always needed the torch to find her way back along the cliff-side path. Her hesitation made the decision for her – she simply could not find it within her to extinguish the light that the torch had created within the prism. She would make her way home one way or another without it.

That night, the little girl slept more soundly than she'd done for months. No awful dreams plagued her, and it was only by the noise of the wind that whistled abrasively through the window pane, and the ferocious lashing rain on the glass, that she was awakened. It was still dark. From outside she heard voices, shouting, and for an instant wondered if in fact she was dreaming. When she heard her father's voice downstairs, she realised she wasn't. What was going on? She jumped out of bed and looked down into the street. Groups of dark figures were gathered there, some with lights or torches in their hands. The wind was howling. There was more shouting. She heard the word 'tanker…'

Her father burst into her room.

'Daddy's got to go out' he said, with an affected calm, but failing to mask the urgency. 'You stay here– '

'But what's happening?'

'Nothing for you to worry about, you just stay here.'

The little girl turned back to her window, after her father had hurried out. The figures were moving off, huddled together against the wind and rain. She saw her father catch up with them, pulling his raincoat on as he went. Further up the street she could see even more figures. They all appeared to be holding torches too. She couldn't make out much more; the rain against the glass distorted everything. They seemed to be heading out past the docks, away towards the cliff-side walk, their torches swaying randomly aloft as they eventually disappeared from view.

The little girl felt a deep and frightening sense of dread. Images from her terrible dream, those horrible, horrible faces, came rushing back to her. She quickly pulled her clothes on over her nightdress, grabbed her old raincoat and raced out after the departing figures.

As soon as she stepped outside the full force of the storm hit her, almost blowing her over. Some figures still lingered, sheltering in various doorways on the main street, mostly women it seemed. The old harbour master's wife was there. She shouted something at the little girl as she ran past her, but she couldn't hear over the noise of the wind, and the crashing of the waves bursting over the harbour wall. She ran and she ran, as fast as she could, out the port and up the cliff-side walk that she had come to know so well.

The group of figures had stopped some way along it. By the time she caught up with them, she was completely soaked through, her breath rasping in her lungs. The storm thundered relentlessly about them. All the men were waving their torches in the air. The little girl didn't understand - what were they doing? She saw her father, his arms too above his head. Some were shouting. Ben was there, so was the mason, the electrician, the carpenter, the burly policeman and even the old school teacher. She squeezed past them, shouting: 'Daddy! Daddy!' He couldn't hear her, only noticing her when she reached up to him, and grabbed onto his coat to steady herself. They were standing so close to the cliff edge – below them the sea seethed and crashed furiously against the rocks.

'Daddy' she shouted, 'Daddy, what's happening?'

He looked shocked to see her. Rain poured over his face as he reached down to lift her up. She pulled back from him. 'What's happening?' she shouted again. He seemed not to know what to say, glancing involuntarily out to the sea. She turned, following his gaze. At first she couldn't see anything, and then, just for a second, there they were: two tiny lights, red and white, blinking and swaying. They were there for a just a moment, and then gone, then they appeared again. She was about to ask, when the sky thundered, a flash of lightning rent the night apart and then she saw it: a huge ship, a tanker! The lightning lasted just long enough to see that the ship was being tossed high on the raging and mountainous waves, only to disappear from view again almost immediately.

She looked up at her father, at the crowd of men waving their torches desperately, their voices hoarse with shouting. It was hopeless. The tanker would never see them.

She pulled on her father's coat. 'Please' she shouted. 'The lighthouse…'

He looked down at her. 'Enough' he shouted back, impatiently. 'Not now!'

'But it can…I'm sure it can. Please…'

She turned to the rest of the men, trying to get their attention.

'The lighthouse' she cried, to each in turn. No-one listened, ignoring her, as they continued vainly to wave their torches overhead.

She looked for Ben, caught his eye, pleadingly. He turned to the doctor.

'You'd best take the li'l miss home Doctor. This is no place for her.'

'I will that Ben. Come along-'

The little girl pulled her hand away sharply. She stood defiantly in front of them. 'No!' she shouted. 'No.' She grabbed at the telescope that Ben held in his hand.

'The lighthouse!' she almost screamed at him, waving the telescope in the direction of the rocky promontory where the lighthouse stood. She couldn't stop the tears from pouring down her cheeks. 'The lighthouse…Ben…please. It can help.'

The old harbour master stared hard at the little girl. She stared back up at him, stubborn and unblinking. Eventually he took the telescope from her hand and put it to his eye.

He looked, and then he looked again. It couldn't be, could it? He looked, again. There was, yes, there was, a glimmer, just the slightest glimmer of a light. 'Well I'll be' he said to himself.

He looked back down at the little girl.

'It just needs ...your help. Please Ben....' she said, her eyes still staring, pleadingly into his.

Ben turned suddenly to the rest of the crowd. 'Right lads, to the lighthouse!' he barked. They looked back confused. 'The lighthouse! C'mon. Now! Bring your lights, all of you, c'mon!' He grabbed some of them, started pulling them with him up the path.

'But-' someone started to say.

'There is a light!' he shouted back, thrusting the telescope into the hand of one of them. 'Look!'

'Oh my God! It's true.' A chorus went up: 'There's a light in the lighthouse!' They all began to stumble up the path, Ben leading the way. He shouted back to the little girl. 'You wait here.'

'I've got her' the little girl's father shouted back.

The little girl huddled up against her father, he with his arm around her, sheltering her as best he could from the howling storm. They watched the group of men disappear into the darkness, picked out only by the swaying points of light from their torches – eventually those too disappeared.

The two of them stood there for what seemed like an age, watching, waiting, the storm raging unabated around them. They must be there by now thought the little girl, but still nothing happened. A fear gripped her, unlike anything she had ever known. She could hardly breathe. She wanted to scream, but she couldn't make a sound. It was all she could do to hold onto her father. The sky thundered and lightning cracked above them, and in amongst it she thought she could hear voices, the pitiful cries and desperate screams of the men trapped, on the stricken tanker. She buried her face into her father's coat. 'They all died.' The lighthouses words echoed in her head. 'They all died.' 'They all died.' They are all going to die, and there was nothing she could do. Nothing.

And then, the night, turned into day.

An unimaginably glorious light burst over their heads, lighting up the whole of the sky. It swept across them, across the cliffs, the rocks, out across the raging sea, disappearing seemingly into the infinite distance. They had to cover their eyes it was so bright. And it swept too across the tanker.

At first the young captain could not believe what he was seeing. Such beams of light, surely they could not be from a lighthouse? But it was true. It was true! The tremendous light lit up everything, the tanker itself, the sea, the towering rocks that until then had only been glimpsed, threatening shadows. And at last the captain had a bearing. He hollered to his first mate and his crew, with frantic hope:

'Hard 'a port lads! Hard 'a port! Keep starboard o' the lighthouse! Hard 'a port!'

It seemed at first as if it was too late, the tanker appearing to stay on its same terrifying course towards inevitable destruction. But gradually and almost imperceptibly its course changed, pulling away from the rocks, to head towards the safety of the harbour.

The weather prevented the tanker from actually docking in the harbour. It weighed anchor just outside, and the ship's crew had to make their way, still somewhat perilously, from the tanker to the harbour in small lifeboats. Climbing, exhausted, onto the quayside, they were greeted by the whole port, all the men returned from the cliffs, the doctor, and his little girl too. The wind still howled, and the rain poured in torrents over them. They were led hurriedly to the tavern, swathed in blankets, and given steaming drinks to warm them, and steady their shattered nerves.

A great clamour of relieved celebration filled the room. The captain's voice rose above it. Holding his mug high, he said: 'On behalf of myself and my crew, I wish to thank the people of this port for the saving of us, for it is as sure and certain as the day is long, we were lost this night, had it not been for you and your lighthouse.'

There was a great cheering, and clapping following the captain's toast.

'T'is not us you should be thankin', capt'n. Not us, not our lighthouse.' Ben's deep and authoritative voice brought a silence to the tavern. 'Neither we, nor it, are responsible for the saving of you and your crew this night.'

'I meant no offence by what I said' the captain replied, mistaking Ben's serious disposition as in some way a criticism of his toast.

'None taken, sir.'

'Well then, friend, please, tell me - to whom should we raise our toast? It cannot be to providence alone that we find ourselves here, safe in your company.'

'Sir, but you are right. It *is* to providence that the saving of you was assured, for it is providence that brought to this port a little girl, and it is to her that you truly owe your thanks.'

'A little girl?' the captain asked, confused.

'Aye sir, a little girl. *This* little girl' He pointed to the little girl, until that moment lost in the throng of people crowding the tavern, still clinging to her fathers coat, shivering despite the blanket wrapped around her shoulders. 'To the bravest little girl I or anyone is e'er likely to know.'

The captain looked from Ben and back again to the little girl. She was so small, so pale, such a slight and delicate thing, and yet, with eyes, that were wide and quite remarkable. He looked back at Ben, who nodded sagely in return. The captain pushed his way through the crowded room to stand in front of the little girl. Kneeling down, he said: 'I do not understand how this can be so, and yet I care not. I am here, saved on all accounts by you, and I thank you, as truly as I or as anyone would, who has faced certain death and been reprieved.' He put out his hand and she, tentatively, hers. 'Thank you' he said again. She smiled ever so slightly.

'But you are freezing' the captain added, looking up.

'I'll take care of her' her father said. The captain nodded, and he, his crew, and everyone else, watched in murmured accord as the little girl's father led her out of the tavern.

He carried her up to her room, undressed her, wrapped her up in his own oversized thick woollen pyjamas, dried her wet hair, and put her to bed.

'You sleep now' he said to her kindly. She smiled the same weak smile back at him. He was looking at her with an expression she had never seen before. Slowly, he bent and kissed her on her forehead. 'I am very proud of you' he said, before turning out her light and closing her bedroom door.

The little girl lay for a while in the dark, but tiredness quickly overcame her – her last memory before she slipped into unconsciousness was of a gentle light sweeping silently and intermittently across her bedroom ceiling.

It was almost inevitable that the little girl, having been caught in weather so inclement and after the rigours of long winter days spent in the lighthouse, once again fell ill. She was confined to her bed for many days, which ultimately extended into weeks. Her father and the harbour master's wife attended to her constantly. Ben visited too. And in her fever she was dimly aware of others, others she couldn't see, but who seemed to surround her on occasion, blessing her with kind hushed voices.

When she finally returned to consciousness, winter had long passed. The lightness of spring filtered through the thin curtains that covered her bedroom window, and she awoke to new sounds, sounds that she'd never heard before. Sounds of chains clanking, banging and hammering, sometimes successions of thumps and louder still, curious horns echoing both far and near, all accompanied by the screeching of many, many gulls. In between, there were endless voices, shouting and constantly laughing and talking. Strange smells too wafted in through her little window, pungent fishy smells. It was all very unusual, but intriguing and intoxicating!

When the little girl had at last the strength to get out of her bed, she parted the curtains, looked out her window, and could hardly believe what she saw. The harbour, full of every ship and vessel you could possibly imagine! She couldn't take it all in! It was incredible – just the way Ben had described it to her, the way it had once been!

When Ben next came to see her, she could hardly contain her excitement.

'Look what's happened Ben? Isn't it wonderful?'

'Aye, I'il miss, certainly is' he smiled at her. 'And all thanks to you.'

'No, no Ben, it wasn't me. It was the lighthouse' she insisted, distractedly, still staring at the panoply of activity in the harbour.

'Well, whatever you say, I'il miss. Certainly the words out, as you can see. Port's a jumpin'!'

'Oh when can I come out, Ben? When?'

'Now you just get your rest. You'll be up and about soon enough. An' I have a wee treat fer ya'. When you feel up to it. A wee walk, perhaps?'

'Oh yes please Ben!'

Some weeks later Ben called upon the little girl, whose health was almost fully returned, and with her father's gracious permission, took her out for the first time since the night of the storm. It was a beautiful bright spring day, and the morning sun bristled warmly over everything.

They walked down the port main street, passing all the shops, every one of them open! They passed too, tavern after tavern, overflowing with men smoking and drinking; the post office, piled so high with packages that the old post mistress struggled to see over; the hairdresser's, filled with customers, shadowy blurred figures seen through its large window completely obscured by condensation; the church, seething with religious fervour, as its congregation sang enthusiastically united with one voice.

In the harbour, ships jostled together, nets and fishing gear piled high on the harbour quay, alongside stacks and stacks of cages and boxes containing all manner of fish and sea creatures. Ben was right: the port was jumpin'! Everywhere people were coming and going – sailors and merchants and fearsome looking whalers, shouting, laughing, and some singing too! And it would be true to say that everyone of them, as they passed, greeted the little girl, doffed their hat, or tugged at a forelock, some even bowed: 'mornin' little miss!', 'you're lookin' well l'il miss', 'good to see you l'il miss.' The little girl was embarrassed by all the attention, but Ben held her hand tightly, thanking them on her behalf.

They finally reached the outskirts of the port, and Ben began to lead her up the cliff-side path. The little girl hesitated, just for a second. 'It's ok l'il mis' he said. 'Ain't nuthin' for you to be afraid of.' He hoisted her onto his shoulders and carried her the rest of the way.

When the lighthouse came at last into view, the little girl felt the same familiar sense of elation that she'd always felt. But something about it was different. She couldn't quite figure out what it was, until they got closer, and then she saw it: the lighthouse was …whiter than it had ever been!

'Ben?' she asked.

'Some of us been busy' was all he said. When they finally reached the lighthouse steps, she saw what he meant. Almost the whole of the outside had been completely painted!

'That's not all' said Ben. 'You go ahead, you 'ave a look. I've still got some things to do out here. You take yer time.'

He pushed the lighthouse door open for her, smiling.

The little girl stepped inside, and immediately as she looked up the stairwell, saw what an incredible change had taken place. Everything, everything that she had not been able to repair, had been fixed! There was glass in all the little windows, the door had had all its splintered panels replaced, the ropes she'd tied around the stair all gone, and as she climbed it, found that it was, for the first time ever, as steady as a rock! She looked into every one of the little rooms, and they too had all been newly furnished, even the little kitchen had been completely rebuilt!

And no matter where she looked, there was not a sign anywhere of the graffiti. Nothing, not a single word remained.

When she reached the top of the stairs, she discovered that all the glass in the lantern light had also been completely replaced. All her hard work...it troubled her, but only briefly, that it had been removed; for looking out through the clear and perfect glass, the view as always was simply staggering!

The prism itself remained exactly as it had been when she'd left it – sitting, massive, if still a little lopsided. She stood and looked at it. It was, so beautiful. So beautiful.

Alone, and in the peace of the lantern light room, she reached out her hand, ever so slowly, towards the prism. And as she did so, as her fingertips were about to touch the prism's sharp and fractured surface...: 'Hello' the lighthouse said.

The little girl could hardly contain her joy at hearing the lighthouse voice again. 'Hello!' she cried back. Tears sprang instantly into her eyes.

'I have missed you' the lighthouse continued, in its familiarly gentle and aged voice.

'Oh I have missed you too!'

'You have been ill?'

'Oh I'm much better now! *Much* better.'

'I am glad.'

The lighthouse seemed to hesitate.

'You have done me immeasurable kindness' it said. 'I have need to thank you-'

'Oh no, no, you don't have to' the little girl interrupted. 'Really you don't. You don't owe me anything. It's enough, really, just being here. Really it is. I-'

'Please', the lighthouse interrupted her, kindly, in return. 'Please. I understand your protestation, but I must. There are indeed many things that I owe you, and in the first instance, I owe you an apology: I am sorry, for I must burden you with my gratitude. I *am* deeply indebted to you, and I must thank you.'

The little girl was about to offer further protest, but it was as if, yet again, the lighthouse had read her mind.

'But my debt is truly a debt of gratitude,' it continued 'which, as such, is bereft of burden, endorsed and shouldered wholeheartedly, willingly. And yet…it remains a debt none the less, and as such demands remuneration.

Others might take some form of worthy action under such circumstances; such is the right and properly demonstrative thing to do. I can only say 'thank you.' 'Thank you' – just two words. It is a feeble recompense. I can strive to imbue these words with a sincerity enough to embellish their worth, to bring some added value to the utterance. I could do that, I *would* do that, and I would repeat these two words, in such fashion, every second of every day if I thought it might make some dent in the debt that I owe you. But it would not, for what I owe you is beyond limit. I owe you everything. Everything.'

'Oh please' the little girl couldn't help but interrupt. 'I only did what I thought was right.'

'Indeed, but to do so, to act upon it, against resistance and in the face of hurt and detraction, is the most immensely courageous of undertakings. It demands sacrifice, and your capacity for sacrifice I have come to appreciate is beyond measure, and indeed, limitless. It is simply remarkable, and truly, inspirational. These are things I have always thought of you, yet may never have said, may never have made proper commendation. If so, this too has been remiss of me. But such a shortfall pales to insignificance, should I fail to make proper expression of the value of your actions: it is beyond measure, beyond words what you, you and you alone, have done for me.

You saved me - the debt is without question deserved, you should not let it trouble you, and yet I know it will - but neither do I need such consequence to justify my desire to protect and defend you. Oh, if there were a mirror I could show you, but really, what need have we ever had of mirrors here? You need only look into your heart and you shall see, for your heart is the truest reflection of my own, and it is there that you can find what it means to me, what you have done *for* me.'

Not for the first time the little girl felt tears trickle down her cheeks, tears though not of sorrow, but tears of warmth, in part at what the lighthouse was telling her, in words tinged with such a raw sentiment, and in part also at the recognition, that the sadness she had always felt lingered behind the lighthouse words, was gone. Its voice had found some curious quality of youth, some spark that until that moment she'd never fully been aware of its absence.

'Look' the lighthouse said, with such a velvet serenity, 'look, look into your heart. You will see that what I tell you is true: you saved me, and by so doing, you need never be afraid again. For if darkness consumes you, a darkness that you cannot dispel, that threatens to overwhelm you, renders you hopeless, lost or alone, look into your heart, and you will find a light there, my light, the light you returned to me. It will lead you from that darkness, without fail, to safety, to a place of shelter, from any storm.'

There was so much the little girl wanted to say, so much she suddenly wanted to ask. But just then Ben shouted up to her:

'Li'l miss? Li'l miss? Time we were getting home.'

'I - I have to go' she said to the lighthouse, in a hushed and apologetic tone.

'C'mon li'l miss – light's a fadin'': Ben again.

'I'll come back, soon as I can. I promise.'

'I will be here' the lighthouse assured, in a voice, as strong now as it had always been kind. 'I am always here.'

'Who ya' talkin' too?' Ben asked, suddenly, from half way up the stairs.

The little girl looked down at him from the lantern light.

'Oh, nobody, nobody. Just to myself' she replied, beaming and wiping away her tears.

The two of them headed back down the cliff-side path, Ben whistling, she skipping alongside him. Every now and then she'd stop and look back, at her beautiful lighthouse, disappearing bit by bit into the distance. Ben chided her – 'it's still there' he kept saying. 'I know', she said, 'I know.'

She took one last look just before it finally disappeared completely from view, at the old lighthouse, standing tall and slender on the rocky promontory, elegant and proud, confronting the sea with such confidence and purpose apparent.

Author's Note: Intermission

THE BIN THAT HAD NO RUBBISH

Once upon a time there was a bin that had no rubbish. The bin was very unhappy that it had no rubbish – all the other bins had tons of rubbish, they were overflowing with the stuff! But this bin had absolutely none, and although the other bins never said so, the bin could tell: they thought the bin, having no rubbish, was no bin at all – in fact, it was a rubbish bin! It could almost hear them saying it, over and over: Rubbish bin! Rubbish bin! Rubbish bin! You're a *rubbish* rubbish bin!

Then, one day: a miracle! The bin's Fairy Binman appeared!

'I'll give you three wishes' the Fairy Binman said, to the bin's tremendous delight.

'Oh I wish, I wish I was full of rubbish!' the bin gushed.

'You sure?' the Fairy Binman asked.

'Yes, oh yes please.'

So the Fairy Binman waved his magic manky glove, and recited:

'Refuse Refuse – do not refuse
To grant this bin its foremost wish
Fill it full up to its lid
Of things discarded and rubbish!'

The next thing the bin knew, it was completely full of rubbish! It was the happiest the bin had ever 'bin'(!). The rubbish was of course somewhat smelly, but it was a small price to pay. At last the bin was the same as the others!

Being filled with rubbish was simply wonderful, but nothing could have prepared the bin for being emptied – my, what a thrill, to be hoisted up into the air and to have its rubbish all tumble out into the bin lorry. Amazing!

The next day, however, the bin was empty again. The bin was terribly sad about this, and called for the Fairy Binman.

'Oh I wish, I wish I was *always* full of the rubbish' the bin implored.

'You sure?' the Fairy Binman asked.

'Oh yes, yes, please.'

So, once again, the Fairy Binman waved his magic manky glove, and recited:

'Refuse Refuse – do not refuse
To grant this bin its second wish
Fill it forever o'er its lid
Of things discarded and rubbish!'

Instantly, the bin was once again full of rubbish! It was wonderful! And, what do you know, when it was emptied, it immediately filled up again. Immediately, no matter how often it was emptied! And now it overflowed with rubbish. The other bins didn't even have a look in – the bin with no rubbish was now for sure the bin with the *most* rubbish!

But as time went on the bin began to get a little sick of being filled with rubbish. The smell was actually pretty horrendous, and some of the things that were thrown away – filthy-disgusting-boggin'-yuuuckkkk doesn't even come close to describing it! And as for being hoisted up and down all the time... it all began to make the bin feel quite sick! The bin realised that it hated being a full rubbish bin! So it called, once again, for the Fairy Binman.

'Please can I use my final wish?'

'Of course' said the Fairy Binman.

'I wish, I wish I was an empty rubbish bin.'

'You sure?' the Fairy Binman asked.

'Yes, oh yes please.'

And so the Fairy Binman, once again, waved his magic manky glove, and recited:

'Refuse Refuse – do not refuse
To grant this bin its final wish
Discard the things beneath its lid
Make an empty bin of rubbish!'

And immediately, the bin's rubbish disappeared. But something did not feel right.

'This isn't right' the bin said to the Fairy Binman.

'What's not right?'

'I don't know – it just doesn't feel right. I don't feel like the way I was.'

'Well you're not' said the Fairy Binman.

'I'm not?' said the bin.

'No, of course not. You're a rubbish bin now.'

'A rubbish bin.......*now*? But I've always been a rubbish bin.'

''Fraid not' the Fairy Binman tutted.

'I wasn't a rubbish bin?'

'Nope.'

'Well what was I then?'

'A recycling bin.'

'A what?'

'A recycling bin. You were a recycling bin.'

The bin hardly knew what to say. It couldn't really believe it.

'I was?'

'Yep'

'Oh......'

Suddenly the bin was very, *very* sad. It didn't like being a rubbish bin, even if it was empty.

'Can I go back to being a recycling bin?' it asked.

'Well I don't see how' said the Fairy Binman, though rather more sympathetically than it might sound. 'Bet you wish you had another wish?'

'Can I?' the bin asked, though admittedly, without much hope.

But, much to the bin's surprise, the Fairy Binman said: 'Of course.' The bin was obviously pleased, but somewhat confused, as you might expect. The Fairy Binman explained: 'Look - I'm only really allowed to grant three wishes, right? But as far as I'm concerned, I wouldn't be much of a fairy if I can't grant wishes, and three just never really seemed enough to me....and anyway, not everyone uses all three. Doesn't seem right to just throw them away. So, if you promise not to tell, I'll give you one more. I've got quite a few spare.'

'Oh yes please' the bin replied.

'Right – what's it to be? And get it right this time.'

'I wish, I wish I was the way I was.'

'An empty recycling bin?'

'Yes.'

'You sure?'

'I'm sure.'

'OK.'

And so the Fairy Binman, for the final time, waved his magic manky glove, and recited:

'Refuse Refuse – do not refuse
To grant this bin its extra wish
Make this bin be as it was
Not an empty bin of rubbish!'

And immediately the bin felt itself to be, once again, the way it had always 'bin' (!!). Except, that is, it didn't bother any more wondering or worrying about what the other bins thought - they were rubbish bins, it was a recycling bin. And from time to time they were all empty..........

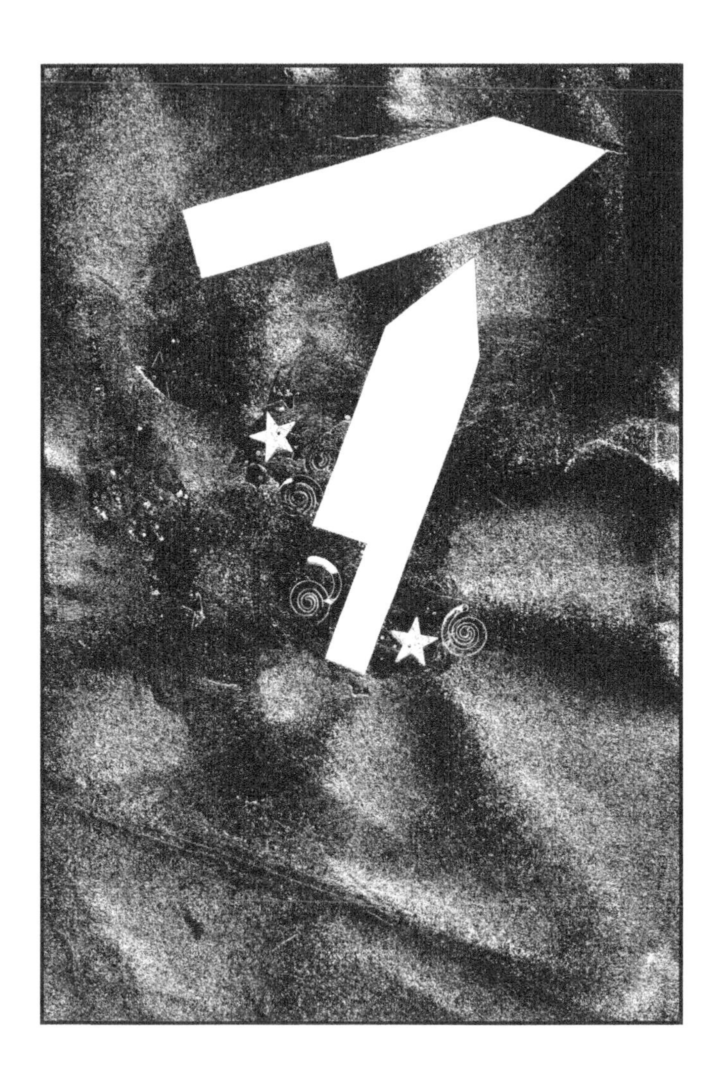

THE RED ROCKET AND THE BLUE ROCKET

Once upon a time there were two rockets – a red rocket and a blue rocket. The two rockets were the absolute best of friends, and they always had been, right from when they had been tiny baby fire crackers! They had grown up together, as neighbours in the small seaside town, where they both still lived. Everyone in the town knew them, and knew how close they were. They were almost like brothers, many thought, and for as long as anyone could remember, the two rockets had rarely, if ever, been seen apart. They were always together, and they always appeared completely happy to be so, forever laughing and joking with each other, kidding each other on and playing contentedly. Not once, *not once*, had they ever been known to have had a fight, or even to have fallen out. Not once. They always agreed, on everything, everything, that is, except for one thing...there was one thing, and one thing only, about which the two rockets *did* disagree: who was the fastest, and this they disagreed on *constantly*!

Aside from each other, the two rockets loved racing more than anything else. They would race literally anywhere, anytime, over anything – it didn't matter. If they were just going for a stroll (well, a fly!) through the town, or through the park, or a trip to the city or to the beach, if they were going for errands, even if they were just going upstairs or even from room to room, they'd race. And whenever there was an actual proper rocket race, a racing competition that is, they would both enter, without fail – they would never miss any opportunity to race, no matter where it was, anywhere in the world: for any opportunity to race was an opportunity to compete, to see who was the fastest!

But the outcome was always the same: sometimes the blue rocket would win, and sometimes the red. It was either one or the other, no one else would even get a look in – they were the two fastest rockets on the planet, for sure!

Yet, afterwards, for days, for months even, the two would bicker over why the one had beaten the other. The racing competitions were of course always the most hotly contested, and their excuses were endless, and often quite ridiculous:

'You only beat me because I wasn't feeling my best that day, you know, I had a cold' one might say.

'A cold? You had a cold? I had a much worse cold than you. I had the flu, and I still won! And you even had the wind behind you!' the other might respond.

'So? You had the wind behind you too! Your fuel was better then mine, that's all it was.'

'Our fuel was the same! I won fair and square. And you even had more people cheering you than me.'

'They were cheering you more! And don't forget, you'd just had a polish.'

'A polish? Don't be ridiculous. Are you saying that a little bit of dust slowed you down?'

'Sure. That, and having the sun in my eyes.'

'The sun was in my eyes too!'

'Well, the sun was worse for me than for you.'

'Rubbish. It was worse for me!'

'No it wasn't – it was worse for me!'

'For me!'

'No, for me!'

'Me!'

'Me!'

'ME!'

'ME!!!'

'ME!!!!'.........

The bickering would go on, on and on and on, neither ever giving in. And it would always end the same way – 'I'll beat you next time' the loser would say. 'Not if I don't beat you first' the other would reply, 'because I'm the fastest.'

'No, I'm the fastest!'

'No, I'M the fastest!!'

'No, I'M the fastest!!'

They'd repeat it over and over and louder and louder and faster and faster, until they couldn't even hear each other anymore, and then they'd collapse in fits of laughter! Anyone who witnessed the rockets' bouts of verbal sparring could have no doubt that, regardless of how much they might squabble and bicker, the two quite obviously loved each other very dearly.

The townspeople were delighted that they had living amongst them the two fastest rockets in the country, in the world even – but, as time went on, they did get increasingly tired of the two rockets incessant bickering (not to mention the constant noise from their engines as they raced by!), despite how good natured it was. It really was getting too much! So the townspeople got together and agreed that what was needed was a resolution, once and for all: who *was* the fastest? If the two rockets couldn't decide, they'd have to do it for them. They therefore arranged a rocket race in their own town: it would be the longest race ever, would go further than any race before, all the way to the moon, and only two rockets would be allowed to enter: their very own red rocket and blue rocket.

The two rockets were delighted when they heard about the race – they chided each other for days beforehand: 'I'll win', 'No, I'll win!', 'No, I'LL win!', 'No, *I'LL* win, because I'm the fastest!'

'No I'm the fastest!'

'No, I'm the fastest!'......as always, they would laugh as they bickered, and now *everyone* got to see. They were interviewed by just about every television station on the planet, and it was always the same, everyone remarking on how much friendship there was between the two rockets, despite how competitive they clearly were.

Eventually, the big day came – all the town came out to watch, as did the whole world! Cameras were everywhere. It was going to be the race of the century!

A huge cheer went up when the two rockets appeared on the launch platform. As the numbers counted down, 10, 9, 8, 7, 6...... the two rockets looked at each other, hugged, and wished each other 'good luck!'

The world held its' breath – 3, 2, 1...BLAST OFF! Another huge cheer erupted as the two rockets lifted off, in a tremendous cloud of fire and smoke.

They raced high into the sky, one minute the red rocket was ahead, just by a nose, the next the blue – and so it went, right into outer space! But just as everyone thought the two were equally matched, slowly, very, very slowly, the red rocket began to pull ahead – the red rocket was winning!

The blue rocket tried as hard as he could to keep up, tried his very best, but the red rocket was just too fast. He was hardly even alongside the red rocket when, all of a sudden… BANG! One of the blue rockets engines exploded! It flung the blue rocket wildly off course, causing his nose to knock into the back of the red rocket!

Well the red rocket couldn't believe it – he hadn't seen the blue rockets engine explode. All he knew was that the blue rocket had knocked into him, trying *deliberately* to throw *him* off course? *Just because he was winning!?* He really couldn't believe it - his friend was cheating! It made the red rocket absolutely furious, and he raced ahead, faster than ever, not even deigning to look back.

'I'll show him' he said, angrily to himself. 'I'm going to beat him by a mile! He'll never beat me! He can cheat if he likes – I'll still be the fastest!'

The red rocket fired all his engines, and by so doing, drowned out any chance of hearing his friend's desperate pleas for help – the blue rocket was now completely and utterly out of control, and was falling back to earth! He cried and cried out for his friend, 'Help me! Help me! Please help me!' but the red rocket, without so much as a backward glance, disappeared further and further up into space.

The world watched in horror as the blue rocket careered in a frightening spiral downwards. Why wasn't the red rocket helping? Surely he'll turn? Surely? But the red rocket just kept going, faster and faster towards the moon – and when he finally reached it, he shouted out ecstatically: 'I win! I win!' But his joy turned to abject terror as he looked behind him – he had expected to see the blue rocket trailing after him. But he wasn't there – he was hurtling unstoppably to the earth!

Author's Note: dun dun duuuuunnnnnn! Two alternative endings follow, for and at the discretion of the reader: for tears, 'The Sad Ending' and for smiles, 'The Not-So-Sad Ending'!

The Sad Ending:

The red rocket tried to catch his friend, tried as best as he could. But his engines were spent, and he simply did not have the power. He watched helplessly as the blue rocket, from such a distance crashed to the earth in appalling silence.

When the red rocket eventually landed back on the planet, he found virtually nothing left of his dear friend the blue rocket. Crowds had gathered around the huge crater where he had crashed. They looked on in silent condemnation as the red rocket stared with eyes blighted by tears, he too, silent, bereft and plagued with guilt.

Nothing was said, as the cameras were one by one turned off, and all the visitors slowly left, the townspeople too – until the red rocket was alone, left sitting in the darkness on the edge of the charred and blackened crater.

'I can never fly again, as you, my friend, are not here' he said to himself, and if any had remained, they would have heard the red rocket add in a voice hollow with a distraught and awful sadness: 'So what use then, is life, without you?'

In the morning the red rocket was found, its engines silent too, like those of the blue rocket, never to be heard again.

Or:

The Not-So-Sad Ending:

The red rocket raced as fast as his engines would carry him – and just as the blue rocket was about to crash into the earth, the red rocket, at the very last moment, caught him!

'Thank you, oh thank you' the blue rocket cried, as the two landed safely back on the ground.

'Please, please don't' said the red rocket. 'I nearly let you die!'

'But I didn't - you saved me!'

'But you could have – and it'd have been all my fault! Please, please forgive me!'

'There is nothing to forgive' said the blue rocket.

'But –'

'No' said the blue rocket, firmly but with the utmost kindness – 'there is nothing to forgive.'

And for once the two rockets did not bicker – the blue rocket was happy to concede that the red rocket was fastest, and the red rocket in turn was happy to concede that the blue rocket was the bestest, the bestest friend anyone could ever have (although, if anyone asked the blue rocket, he would tell you the red rocket was the bestest..............)

Tock Tock Tock Tock
Tock Tock Tock Tock
Tock Tock Tock Tock

THE CLOCK THAT COULD NOT TICK

Once upon a time there was a clock that would not stop tocking. That's all the clock did, all day long – tock tock tock. It drove all the other furniture nuts.

'I wish you'd stop tocking' they'd plead, imploring the clock, again and again, at times in jest, but mostly in frustration and sometimes, in complete and utter desperation!

The clock would apologise, quite sincerely, and he would promise that he would try his very best to stop. But he just couldn't – without any malice whatsoever, he would simply carry on tocking regardless – tock tock tock tock tock tock.......

'It never stops!' the other pieces of furniture would complain bitterly to each other. 'I wish he would shut up!' they'd whisper, and they felt bad for wishing it, because they liked the clock, but the tock tock tocking was becoming unbearable. They decided that something just had to be done.

They did, however, have a bit of a problem - none of them knew anything about clocks, or how they worked. So they agreed that they would have to consult an expert. The clock-maker would have to be called in (actually the furniture had no idea what a clock maker was, but the side-board reassured them that she had heard of such a person, and the others were happy to take her word. She, after all, had the worst of it, as the clock was nearest to her. Actually he sat right on top of her!)

A note was therefore hastily put together:

Dear Maker of the Clocks

We have a clock that tock tock tocks.
Please can you make the tocking stop?

Yours truly,
The Furniture

The note was brief, but to the point, and, keeping in mind of course just how difficult it is for furniture to write, really quite an accomplished piece, which made the furniture justifiably proud!

It was not however, such a pleasant occasion, the day the clock-maker came. The furniture couldn't bring themselves to watch, as the back of the clock was unceremoniously wrenched open, and awful looking instruments inserted, obviously instruments of cruelty and torture, as a dreadful grinding and horrendous scratching ensued. It was terrible to hear, simply terrible, but, with one last rasping '*boooiiiiiiiinnng*', it was finally done – the tock tock tocking was stopped!

The pieces of furniture were overjoyed. Silence at last! That night, for the first time ever, they all slept soundly, so soundly in fact that they all slept in! The remainder of that day, what was left of it, was absolutely wonderful too! They chatted away without interruption, and so happily that they lost all track of time, getting to bed terribly late!

Again that night, they slept soundly, and, again, they slept in! But they chatted away uninterrupted the next day as happily as they had the day before, despite being awfully tired from their late night. They had to admit, this chatting was really quite exhausting, but they all still agreed how wonderful it was that the tocking had stopped.

But the next day came and went in a bit of a blur – they all woke up at different times, and those that were awake found that they had much less to say to each other, having pretty much exhausted most of their conversation over the previous two days. And so it was the following day, and the next, and the next, until one day, some few weeks after the tocking had been stopped, the furniture found that they had absolutely nothing left to say to each other.

And, to make matters worse, they were all very confused too, as no-one had any idea what time of day it was. The clock appeared to have stopped altogether!

'I wonder what's wrong' they said to each other. They asked the clock, but it just sat there, in silence, apparently ignoring them.

'I think he's in the huff' the side-board suggested. But they knew instinctively that that wasn't it – something was clearly very wrong.

'We'd best get the clock-maker' they agreed, and so another note was hastily put together:

Dear Maker of the Clocks

Our tocking clock now has stopped -
Please can you fix our broken clock?

Yours truly,
The Furniture.

The clock-maker came that very day. He examined the clock for some time, and then pronounced his verdict: 'Your clock cannot tick' he said, matter of factly.

'Is there anything you can do?' the furniture asked.

'I'm afraid not' he said. 'I cannot make him tick. I can only make him tock.'

'And if he tocks, will he work again?'

'Most certainly' said the clock-maker. 'But he will tock tock tock as he did before, if that is your decision.'

The pieces of furniture all looked at each other, rather perplexed.

'Thank you' they said. 'We'll let you know.'

After the clock-maker had left, the pieces of furniture sat around in an awkward and embarrassed silence. Eventually one of the chairs said, meekly, and to no-one in particular: 'I never noticed that he didn't tick.'

'No, me neither' said the others, just as meekly, and also rather sheepishly. They sat in silence for a while longer.

It was the wardrobe who, in a voice much less pompous and authoritative than was his norm, finally suggested: 'Perhaps...perhaps we might invite the clock-maker back?'

'You mean...to fix the clock?' offered the chest of drawers.

'Yes, well, yes, just for a trial mind....?'

There was a general consensus, evidenced in a chorus of sombre 'yesses', and another note was hastily, (and if any of the furniture had been asked, quite sincerely), put together:

Dear Maker of the Clocks,

We're sorry that we stopped our clock.
Please can you make him tock tock tock?

Yours truly,
The Furniture.

And so it was, that when the clock was fixed and once again, tock tock tocking away, the other pieces of furniture were grateful to be able resume their daily routine, albeit with rather less complaint, as they listened with a newly discovered contentment to the endless tock tock tocking of the clock that could not tick.

THE CLOCK THAT COULD NOT TOCK

Once upon a time there was a clock that would not stop ticking. Tick tick tick. That's all it did, day and night. It drove the old lady crazy.

Regardless of where she was in her big rambling old house, no matter what she was doing, the sound of the clock would always be there, incessantly tick-tick-ticking away. She could be in her enormous kitchen, reheating leftovers in her equally enormous battered pots; in the draughty wash room out back, ironing her delicate and increasingly faded lace handkerchiefs; in the icy cold black-and-white tiled bathroom, dutifully bathing in the brown stained iron bathtub; or in the dust covered conservatory, tending to her rather pathetic selection of flowering plants - regardless, wherever or whatever she was doing, it would not matter, there the ticking would be – tick tick tick tick tick tick, endless ticking, tick tick tick ticking away.

She could try and drown it out: with the radio, humming quietly along with tunes from her youth, memories flooding back as she did so; or with the television, although she found most of the programmes difficult to follow (and many were *so* violent!) despite being able to hear them so much better with the volume turned up; or even with her trusty hoover, although she increasingly felt less and less inclined to clean and only did so for the distraction from the tick tick ticking. But nothing worked – the tick tick ticking would always be there, tick tick ticking away, in the background.

'Shut up, shut up. Shut up!' she longed to say, but she never did. She went about her daily business as best she could, trying to ignore the clock's terrible irritation.

The days were bad, but worst of all were the nights. When the old lady tried to get to sleep – tick tick tick tick tick – can you imagine it? She would bury herself under the blankets, pull a pillow up over her head, and say to herself: 'Tomorrow, tomorrow, I'm going to do something about this. I *will* do something. I can't stand this any more!'

But, tomorrow would come, and the old lady would look at the clock, still ticking away, and her resolve would fail her – it was such a beautiful thing, standing there, so elegant and proud, and yet, so delicate and fragile too. 'I can't do it' she would say to herself. 'Maybe tomorrow. And anyway, today might not be so bad.'

And so it would go on, day after day, month after month, year after year, the old lady getting older still, and every day enduring the same irritation, her frustration mounting as every night making the same promise to herself and every morning failing to see it through.

Then one day, as she sat, (tick tick tick tick tick) trying to (tick tick tick tick tick) read, quietly (tick tick tick tick tick) in the study, suddenly (TICK TICK TICK TICK TICK) she had had enough. Something snapped - the old lady threw down her book, and ran blindly from the study, into the great empty hall where the clock stood, its terrible ticking echoing throughout the whole house. TICK TICK TICK TICK TICK TICK......

'Tick, tick, tick, that's all you do! I wish you'd stop, I wish you'd stop ticking!' she screamed at the clock. 'I wish you'd stop!!!' she screamed and screamed, over and over, and she beat her frail and bony, veined little hands helplessly against the clock's hard wooden surface. 'Stop! Stop! STOP!' she howled, and she ran up to her bedroom, threw herself onto the bed and collapsed, sobbing: 'stop, stop – please stop......'

When the old lady awoke the next morning, her eyes bleary and red, something was strangely different. She sat up and tried to understand what it was, what was it? And then she realised, what it was: silence. The ticking had stopped.

She listened as hard as she could, thinking maybe the ticking was just very quiet, maybe, but it was true – the ticking *had* stopped. She got up, pulled her nightgown around her, and wandered out from her bedroom. It was quiet everywhere.

She went into every room, but there was not a sound, nothing. Finally she arrived in the hall – and it was same there too. Nothing. She crept up to the clock and pressed her ear against it. Still, nothing. She stood back and looked at the clock, waiting and waiting for the ticking to start again, but it didn't. There was only silence.

And as she stood there, staring and waiting, she noticed something about the clock she hadn't noticed before. 'My, but how finely carved it is' she thought to herself. Had it always been so? She couldn't remember. Perhaps.

The old lady went about all her usual chores that day, waiting and waiting for the ticking to start again – but it never did. She hummed along with the same tunes on the radio, some of the melodies seeming sweeter than she remembered them, and she even managed to watch the television that evening, without feeling the need to turn up the volume as she had done so often in the past. 'My, how wonderful are subtitles!' she discovered.

And when she went to bed that night, for the first time in so long, longer in fact than she could remember, she slept, peacefully, from the moment she laid her head on her pillow.

In the morning she awoke, fully expecting the ticking to have started again – but it was still the same. Nothing. She checked the clock, listened closely up against it once more – nothing. She ran her hands over its worn surface, picking out even more of the clock's delightful little carved details. Had those fine twists and turns always been there? She ran the tips of her fingers along the gentle contours of the clock face, and felt her heart warming in ways long forgotten. It truly was a beautiful clock.

As every day then went by, the old lady discovered more and more things about the clock she'd never noticed before, things likewise long forgotten? She couldn't remember - had it always been so, she wondered - how elegantly the clock was shaped and carved, how tall it stood, proud certainly, but my, how rich and luxuriant was its wooden finish, of numerous shades of browns and hues of red and even gold threaded throughout, how keen and sharp were its black hands, how striking was the calligraphy of the equally black as night numbers etched into the marble white face, how marvellously it was all engineered, its workings so refined and carefully composed, how well crafted were those tiny cogs and wheels, how snugly the big brass key fitted into the brass winder. And the gentle curve of the glass face, over which she now never tired of running her fingertips, how delightfully and softly it swung open on its tiny brass hinges. How could anyone have constructed something of such exquisite beauty she wondered? It was so perfect, in every way! And such was the joy and wonder of these daily re-discoveries, the old lady became oblivious to and completely unconcerned that the clock's hands no longer moved.

As if in some delightful conspiracy, every day too her house seemed different - the sunlight seemed to shine more brightly into every room, colours that had once seemed faded and dull became brighter too, vivid and luminous; the heating, which she had always found to be somehow insufficient, all of a sudden seemed to fill the whole house with a generous and embracing warmth (she had always been so cold!). Even the aroma from her small selection of plants seemed to perfume every room, abundantly with their rich evocative fragrance - so many things, so many things she'd never seen before, never smelt or touched, suddenly everything in her whole house seemed different, vibrant and alive.

And so the old lady lived, happily ever after, seeing out the rest of her life until the day she died, in the comfortable silence of her house, where every day she discovered more and more things to wonder at and delight in, content and alone but for the company of her clock that did not tock.

THE BEAUTIFUL COAT

'Tis true: there's magic in the web of it.

WILLIAM SHAKESPEARE, 'OTHELLO'

Once upon a time, there was a little boy who lived in a vast and great, dark city. He, together with his friends, loved to play in the streets of the city, incessantly, to skip and run, laughing, carefree and careless through its stony corridors. They were a wild and fearless pack, he and his friends, unassailable, their antics and irreverent attitude made tolerable by their youth, their innocence and by the cut of their shorts.

It seemed to them that time stood perfectly still in the city – no years passed, nor months, nor weeks, nor even days! Never were there different seasons, neither were there even different times of the day – there were no mornings, no afternoons, never was it time to go to bed or time to get up for school. It was always...evening, an impeccable, humid summer evening, when the day had at last irrevocably receded, the city fixated on that moment when the sky becomes coloured by unfathomable purples, ambers and reds, and the questionable possibilities of the night remain intrigues, yet to be revealed.

Memory paints a different picture than reality – the night-time must surely have eventually come, as must have, inevitably, the day, and with it, facades dissolved to reveal unavoidable truths: the streets the boys inhabited were in fact mean, dangerous places, dirty and full of desperate hopes. But it made no difference to them; they were immune to the implications of reality, sheltered and protected as they were by the warmth of the evening glow and the invincibility of childhood. Where darkness loitered, in the city's gloomy corners and shadowed doorways, the little boy, like the other boys, saw only glorious colours in the dubious shades. He fabricated adventure from menace. Smells, even the rank, fetid ones, perfumed in his mind; and from the apartments over-head, where indistinct voices might be raised in resentful and bitter argument, it would appear as if they sang out, harmoniously and soft through the open yellowed windows. Shouts and screams would become melodious laughter, and all of it merged with the horns and scrapes of the parading traffic below to create a kaleidoscope of a world, rich, fragrant and delightful.

The whole scene captivated all the boys, unreservedly: as their palace of dreams, made real, in the diversity of its distractions, it offered, comparatively, a freedom wherein they shared an intimate and communal sense of belonging, safe in its impartial embrace, secure, comforted and perpetually encouraged.

No constraints were ever applied to their behaviour - the city accommodated their impudent acts, and in fact, provoked their natural capacity for anarchic irresponsibility. They would career through its streets, colliding with neighbours and strangers alike, hindered only in their chaotic progress by the density of the street-life around them, as they squeezed between the legs of the market stalls and the dented fenders of bulbous brightly coloured cars, their figures distorted deliriously in the hubcaps and chrome as they passed.

All the while they would be shooed and chided salaciously by adult voices, some gravelled and laced with beer and tobacco, some shrill and piercing, some stern, others well meant and caring - regardless, the invigorating pulse of the city stimulated distractions too enticing for the boys to take any heed, a pulse that emanated primarily from the luxuriously diverse panorama of shops and bars that lined the city streets.

The bars of course were the forbidden places, fearfully demarcated as such that only the older children dared enter. In consequence it was the shops, by the immediacy of their attraction, which fostered the greatest fascination, especially to the youngsters in the group, of which the little boy was one. Consistently bright lights, some sparkling, some sharp, pointed and direct, some unforgiving, pale blue washes of fluorescent illumination, would spill unconditionally from the expansive shop windows, inviting them to stare at the various wares displayed there, displays that were hypnotically resplendent with all manner of realised desires: obscure mechanical gadgets that spoke of secret and confidential adventures; raw, and implausibly bloodless meats impaled on killer hooks; multicoloured spirals of sugary sweets and candies; swollen breads and swirling pastries, seductively glazed in honey and festooned with exotic fruits; tiny jewels and clumsy diamonds, of distressing and incomprehensible value; displaced rugs and drapes and candlesticks and empty birdcages; endless rows of magazines full of captivating images of glamour and other worlds; and all of it resplendent with facts and figures, unremittingly demanding their attention, of the boys and every passer-by. Signs and statements, offering deals too tempting to ignore, were plastered across every shop window, above which the shop names boldly proclaimed and determined the independent character and intention of each establishment.

It was, in all, an obscene cacophony of commercial endeavour; an almost endless selection of *things* which assaulted the little boys, creating a fantasy-world that contained all their possible futures, a distant secret adult world that they could invade, take pleasure in its vicarious delights, without means, and without reward other than the thrill from some blatant yet harmless pilfering. One day it would all be theirs, this world of commerce and goods, all the things in it would become available to them, readily accessible without resort to distraction, tactic or enticement – and by being so, its enthralling quality to intrigue their young minds would evaporate. But for now, these shops presented such a provocative landscape, vibrant, and so full of amazement, that it provided endless fuel for their fertile imaginations, and satisfied and indulged their limitless capacity for entertainment and amusement, wherein they could busy themselves in their ridiculous, interfering yet innocuous games.

Outwardly, the little boy did not shrink from the unfettered indulgence in such common games. He shared equally with his friends in all the pleasures that the city proffered. In fact he would often become entirely consumed by the city, and completely lost in the wonder of it. He would assume that the others were as lost too, that they saw it as intensely as he did, and that they were as consumed as he. He didn't, indeed he couldn't, know that this was not the case. *His* capacity for passion was considerably greater than theirs, but he was so young, and by his inherent immaturity, by his attendant lack of experience simply of living, it was a comparison impossible for him to make.

If there were a more concrete inkling in his young mind that he was in some way different, it was not made manifest to him by this forgivable mistake of interpretation – rather it was because, the little boy had a secret.

It was a secret, unique, to him alone, and not shared by the others. There was one particular shop to which the little boy would go, a very special shop that his friends neither knew of, nor if they did, showed no interest in. The shop was down a peculiarly secluded little side street, away from the busy streets where the boys usually played, in a much quieter part of the city, less patterned and much less colourful. Actually it was more of a lane than a street, narrow, winding, and lined in high blank rough stone walls, which, although making the lane considerably darker, dangerous even, made it in turn also curiously enticing.

There were no shops down this lane, other than the one that attracted the little boy, no shops other than this one tiny boutique. Its solitary presence alone might have accounted for the spell that this shop held for the boy, and it certainly was a delightful shop in its own right: a single bowed bay window protruded small glass panes subtly outwards, flanked by a similarly ornately carved glazed door. All of it was painted in a sharp and bright white finish, so clean and so at odds with the grim surroundings: by its unique brilliance, it seemed to the boy as if the shop were an unrivalled star, uncommonly stationary, persistent and enduring in an unforgiving pitch black sky.

Regardless though of the fascination that the shop itself held for the boy, it was not that which drew him to it. Rather it was the single item hanging in the shop window: a glorious, golden coat.

He would stop for what seemed like uncharted hours in front of the shop window, scared to be seen, but unwilling to leave, unwilling, indeed, unable, to withdraw his gaze from the coat. It was truly the most beautiful thing the little boy had ever seen: a long slendrous garment, all of it, every inch of it, gold, every part, from the thin beading on the collar, the generous vents and upturned cuffs to the delicate interwoven stitching, to the double row of worthy buttons down the front, the wholesome pockets, the modest lapels. Each was a golden shade, perfectly composed against the backdrop of a golden material so exceptionally rich, and so luminous that it seemed to the boy it must have been cut from the sun itself. The boy's own garments were hewn from rough and drab cloth, featureless, and always deficient in some way - too long or too short, too loose or too tight, itchy and uncomfortable. But this coat was simply perfect - perfectly tailored, perfectly shaped, perfectly made and crafted. Nothing the boy had ever seen could compare to its beauty and perfection - a radiant golden light almost seemed to emanate from the coat, to shine through the small glass panes of the bay window, caressing him, all over his whole body, his face, his hands, through him, inside and out.

And as he stood, enveloped in the coat's golden glow, the boy would picture the day when, having earned money enough to purchase the coat, doubtless, he imagined, a ridiculously excessive amount of money (for surely an item as wonderful as this must be incredibly expensive!), he would step confidently, into the shop, pay graciously for it, and he would put it on, knowing with an absolute certainty that it would fit him as perfectly, without need for any alteration or adjustment.

In his exquisite fantasy he knew, with the same certainty, that this coat would be the only coat he would ever need - a coat that would keep him warm in the cold of winter, but would be light enough to wear casually in the summer, would complement anything he would ever choose to wear, and would be appropriate for every event and occasion. And when he did not have need to wear the coat, he would not put it away hidden in some dark, airless closet, but rather he would display it openly, proudly letting it hang in his home, for all to see. It would be his greatest possession, his most valued treasure and he would want everyone to know it, to envy him his great fortune: to be the possessor of such an incredible belonging.

He felt all these things and more, in his intoxication. But there was something else, a feeling deep in his heart, an instinct he could not explain nor put into words: somehow he knew that this coat, by some inalienable right, was his. It was an unfounded belief, but unshakeable, a vague but definite certainty, as if it was deserved of him, a justifiable entitlement: one day, one day he would own this coat, and from that day, he would no longer be the weak little boy that he often felt himself to be. Instead, he would be strong, smart, handsome, and unafraid, at last unassailably grounded and confident in a world that often left him vulnerable and confused, if only because of his secret and all consuming passion for this golden edifice.

His passion was an innocent passion, but, nonetheless, the little boy's secret musings down the dark lane were accompanied by a delicate and difficult shame. It confounded him into a comfortable solitude - he never told anyone about the coat, or the feelings that it provoked in him. Any noise in the lane would cause him to hide, to run quickly away. But whenever he could, whenever it was safe, if he was sure he was alone and nobody had followed him, he would return, always with the same delirious expectation, his heart sick with trepidation and delight, drawn by the golden glow from the tiny boutique window - to stand and stare at the beautiful coat that would one day be his.

Time passes in the city. The city changes, it rises and it falls, the colours change, the shapes change, the materials of which the city is made change, and all the shops change with it. The boy plays with the others throughout these changes, often feeling them more than seeing them – it is a slow but continual transformation, measured only by the regularity of the boy's secret visits to stare in private contentment, at the golden coat.

But, little by little, his visits to the small shop lessen. The changes around them all, take him away from that part of the city. He passes the lane less often, has less opportunity to be there, has less time to linger in his treasured moments of silent adoration. He forgets from one time to the next when he was last there, until eventually he forgets how to even find the small shop. But he isn't sad about it. Other things become important to him - the new city has new things to enjoy, and all boys together, they re-invent their games, they change with the city, become white when it is white, take on its hues, its moods and intentions.

He never forgets the coat, never forgets the sense of inevitability that it will one day be his, but, as he drifts unquestioningly with the others through the changing background of the city, his future more choosing him rather than him choosing it, the memory of his deep desire begins to fade.

Time passes again, and with it, reality and memory blur. One day, when the boy is older, he has at last money enough to buy the coat. But he cannot find the small shop; in fact he does not even try. It actually doesn't even occur to him. There are other shops now, other boutiques, full of all sorts of coats. He picks one out, a coat that seems to be as likely the one that he had so desired, once, so long ago. He buys it, and is shrouded in it, happy for a while in its golden, or nearly golden, hue.

Time passes again, much more time, and the boy doesn't realise it, but he owns many coats, sees many come and go, some keeping him warm, some not so warm, some lovelier than others, some more expensive than others, some that fitted well, others that didn't. They all hang in his closet, some worn and moth eaten, shredded, discarded, others newer, cleaner, sharper, and others, many others, often more functional than any are beautiful. None of them though is the golden coat, *the* golden coat, and the memory of those precious moments spent enveloped in its golden glow recedes finally to the point where they seem to the boy like snapshots from a dream.

Eventually he can no longer recall the desire that he felt. Whenever he tries, the feelings he had all appear impossibly elusive and intangible, and ultimately he is convinced that it was no more than a foolish imagining of childhood, an illusionary fantasy, that was not, and never would be, real. His hope, his trust, in the absolute belief that the coat would one day be his, is irrevocably lost and forgotten.

It is only by chance, one day, many, many years later, the boy, admittedly not a little boy any more, but a boy nonetheless, is wandering, alone and un-distracted through the city streets, and he finds himself, once again standing in front of the small boutique window. And there, in front of him, is the golden coat.

Time, in an instant, seems to stop. The boy can only stare in disbelief, dumbfounded by the discovery and stunned into immobility. He cannot comprehend what he is seeing, cannot believe that what is hanging in front of him is the same coat - the same coat? Questions tumble through the boy's mind - can this be true? Can this be the same coat? How could it be? There is no mark upon it, no diminishment in any way - if anything it appears even more beautiful than it was!

But as the coat's radiance enfolds him again, undeniably the same, so golden and so wonderful, his desire, so long forgotten, is re-awakened, assaulting him with an unexpected vigour. The world dissolves completely around him, leaving him to stare in a silent but delightful communion, and in his amazement, as a resounding and untamed joy fills his heart, a single thought overwhelms him: my dream was real!

It is only by the tinkling of the shop bell that he is roused from the spell. His eyes re-adjust to the reality of the world again, and with it, the years of his age suddenly seem to weigh down heavily upon him. A weariness descends on the boy, strange thoughts and anxieties confound him, and for a second he hesitates - this coat cannot be for someone like me, he thinks - it must be for another, for someone younger, more agile, fitter and stronger.

But as quickly as his doubts assail the boy, they are in turn assuaged, as a gentle calm settles on him. Standing in the coat's glowing presence, something, he can't explain what exactly, comforts him. It is as if a soothing breath washes over him, and his doubts somehow vanish. He remembers the fear he once had, that he might be seen standing so, like this - but that fear too leaves him. For the first time ever, he is not scared. And when, before, he had never even dared contemplate entering the shop, now he does so with a casual ease. Perhaps such ease might have been ascribed to the door being left invitingly ajar. Perhaps - but regardless, it was as if he were being taken by a small hand, he steps from the lane into the shop, the shop bell tinkling again clear but distant, and he is led, entranced, to stand within inches of the golden coat. Time stretches out in front of him, he is reaching out, slowly, so slowly, his fingers uncurling and extending in front of him, in a moment to touch his dream......

A voice from behind interrupts him: 'Can I help you sir?'

The boy turns with a start, to see an old man, bent and hunched over a steel cane, with blank, watery eyes staring at him from under knotted brows and delicate reading glasses. A tailor's measuring tape hangs loosely over his shoulders, although the boy need not have had such a clear indication of the old man's profession. Something about his attire generally, his persistently fine suit, worn though and faded, swathed in an oversized cardigan, his fingerless gloves, his gnarled arthritic hands, and his posture too, of a disposition inclined naturally to imperious deference. Every aspect of the old man's countenance confirmed it: a tailor.

In a voice stronger than the body would suggest, the old tailor asks him again.

'Can I help you?' the hand not grasping the cane reaching out.

'This coat...?' the boy replies, with a hesitant gesture to the coat hanging in the window.

'The golden coat?' the old tailor asks.

'Yes' says the boy. 'How much is it?'

'Oh, I'm afraid that coat is not for sale' the old tailor replies, matter of factly, and not unkindly but resolutely.

The words, and the manner and abruptness of their telling, fall on the boy like a stone. All the joy he had felt evaporates, and his heart sinks, pulled down by a sense of impenetrable loss and longing combined. He can only muster in response an involuntary 'oh -' as he looks back in a desperate silence at the old tailor. The old tailor says nothing, returning the boy's look openly, but blankly still, with no offer of compensation let alone solace in his demeanour.

Eventually and without conviction the boy repeats the old tailor's words: 'Not for sale?' he says, quietly and as pointlessly and empty of influence as an echo is.

'No' replies the old tailor, still kindly but firmly. 'No' he says again, adding a concessionary 'I'm sorry'.

The words, in their small comfort, as if in acknowledgement of the depth of the boy's apparent loss, spark a resolve in him, a resolve he truly did not know he had, but doubtless forged from years of resilience to the demands of his passion. He could turn and leave, as he'd so often done in the past - but regrets flood his memory, of chances lost, opportunities missed, dreams he sacrificed for the benefit of others before himself. It causes a revolt in him: I cannot leave, he says to himself, I cannot, I cannot. The coat, *my* coat, is here, now, it is within my reach. He is compelled to persist, and asks: 'Perhaps...could I perhaps, just try it on?'

'But certainly' says the old tailor, with an unexpected lightness. 'Please...' he adds, as he indicates with his gnarled hand for the boy to turn around. A feeling of such intense trepidation fills the boy as the tailor helps him remove his own coat, standing then for seconds, seconds that seem to extend to an age, as the tailor behind him lifts the coat from the mannequin, and then......the golden coat slides over his body like a wave. He is instantly lost in it, transported to some other world he could hardly have imagined. Although still unquestionably in the shop, suddenly everything in it seems to have been completely transformed, and to have taken on a shimmering and magical golden hue! The golden radiance that had always appeared to emanate *from* the coat, to surround him and him alone, now seemed to encompass *everything*! And in a manner too of such unbelievable comfort - never had the boy felt such comfort! It was as if the boy's own body, every limb, every fibre of his own physical being, was somehow subtly changed, transformed to fit exactly to the coat's own fine contours. How was it possible that any garment could feel as luxurious as this, and protective too? Where he had imagined the coat might be light upon him, and it certainly was, it also seemed to host a firm steeliness in its velvet fabric. It was like being shrouded in a feather coat of armour.

All the materials of the world must have been brought to bear to create such a garment, or a material from some other unknown yet hallowed and mystical place, so unique was the sensation of wearing it. Such...perfection – it was simply impossible to describe, impossible almost to believe that such perfection could actually be real!

'Well?' the old tailor asks the boy.

'It's so...... perfect' the boy replies, feeling at once the inadequacy of his words, and yet without recourse to any other. 'I never thought it would be..... *so* perfect.'

'Well, yes', says the old tailor. 'Yes, yes, of course', as he smoothes the coat down over the boy's shoulders. 'Why would it not be?'

Something about the old tailor's words confuse the boy.

'I don't understand..?' he says. 'The coat–'

'Is your coat' says simply the old tailor.

'What do you mean?'

'It is your coat'.

'My coat?'

'Yes, your coat – it was made for you. For you, only for you.'

The boy feels tears suddenly well up in his eyes, but he is confounded still, and can't seem to comprehend what the tailor means. In his confusion, the stagnancy of the life he had led catches him up, stalling him. 'But...it is not for sale?' he repeats, clumsily and consequently pragmatic.

'No, no, of course not – how could it be? No one else could possibly own this coat. No one else could possibly wear it. It has been here, waiting for you...it is yours – it always has been.'

'But...?'

'Please' the old tailor says, his eyes, at once luminous and blank, but with a glow too of intimate warmth and tender generosity lending an implication to the words again repeated, a clarity impossible for the boy to mis-comprehend: 'This coat is yours. It is yours, and no one else's. It always has been, and it always, always, will be.'

Something inside the boy's heart just breaks. Tears, a whole flood of tears, a lifetime of tears, welled up and damned, suddenly are released. They spill helplessly down his cheeks, tears that, try as he might, the boy cannot stop. He stands, pathetically but shamelessly crying, wrapped up still and warm in the golden coat's embrace.

When at last the boy's tears subside, the old tailor pats him softly on the arm, smiling gently.

'Careful there' he says, 'don't want to ruin it'.

He helps take the coat from the boy's shoulders, to replace it over the mannequin in the shop window. The boy watches him, dumbly mute, suddenly exhausted and utterly drained. Ignoring the boy, the old tailor fusses quietly about, as he tidies the shop, opening and closing the slender, polished timber drawers lining the walls, overflowing with all manner of garments, shirts, ties, socks, braces. He constantly disappears back and forth between the shop front and what the boy realises must be a workroom in the back, where he catches glimpses of a room packed with all sorts and types of fabrics and cloths, countless rolls of them, and other mannequins too, some partially clothed, others less so. The old tailor takes a little time to adjust them, and also to rearrange various items - cufflinks and tie pins - in the small glass topped counter near the shop door.

Once the shop is tidied to the old tailor's satisfaction, he lights a fire in the grate of a small fireplace, set discreetly in an alcove between the shop front and the workroom in the rear. He indicates to the boy to sit in one of the two ornate armchairs arranged on either side of it. The boy settles into one, the old tailor opposite him in the other.

They sit for a while in companionable silence, until, with his strength and composure returned, the boy asks: 'Who made the coat? Did you?'

'Yes, yes, I did. A long, long time ago now' the tailor says. 'So long ago….' The words fade away, the old tailor's head looking sideways for a moment, his attention gone. He comes back as abruptly from his momentary musing. 'Is it as fine as I remember? It has been a while since I've seen it, properly. I believe I had quite an eye.'

'It is ….glorious' says the boy. His eyes rove across the coat, picking out continually more and more delightful little details, things that he had not been able to see from outside, obscured as they had been by his restricted view through the window. Curiously, the coat was more worn than it had seemed, in places slightly creased and marked – and yet, such details only served to endear the coat to him more, made it even more perfect, enhanced by the boy's unmitigated acceptance of these so called imperfections.

'It is beautiful' he says.

The old tailor smiles – 'I remember it so…my eyes…'

He lets the words hang, and in the silence the boy looks at him. Such an old, old man, and everything about him wrinkled. Everything, his face, his hands, his grey hair too, what is left of it, all curled up, his clothes too, everything, wrinkled,

wrinkled and in turn so unavoidably indicative of the tailor's great age - and yet, somehow, despite the fact, despite the absence of any indication of any remnant whatsoever of youth in the old tailor's appearance, he exuded some strange sense of permanence. He moved slowly, talked slowly, but there was a firmness, a deliberateness, in his movements and in his words. It was a somewhat confounding apparition, but no more so evidenced than in the old tailor's eyes – they looked back at the boy as if they were looking right through him, and yet it is as if they were blank too, blind even. The boy cannot help but find it disconcerting, and looks away.

'Can I…can I take it?' he asks, glancing towards the coat.

'The coat is yours' replies the old tailor. 'You can do with it as you please.'

The boy hesitates, not sure what to do or say.

'Or you can leave it here if you prefer?' the old tailor suggests.

'Can I?'

'Of course. It'll always be here. And perhaps it's for the best, today at least – the weather?'

The little boy hadn't noticed, until the tailor pointed it out – outside a terrible storm was raging! Driving sleet and rain was pouring torrentially, from a dark, thunderous sky turned ominous and foreboding. A predatorial gloom hung over everything, threatening almost to consume them - it seemed to the boy that only the golden glow from the coat protected them. Or was it perhaps the light from the fire? For a second he isn't sure.

'It's a good coat, certainly,' says the tailor, 'but perhaps this is not the best weather for it? You can visit any time you like' he adds.

'Yes' agrees the boy, at once reluctant and relieved. 'Yes, if that's ok?'

'Certainly' the old tailor re-assures him. 'Any time you like.'

'Well ok, I'll come back tomorrow.....?'

The old tailor nods his assent, and without any further discussion, the boy takes his leave, stopping only to look briefly at the coat, afraid suddenly to touch it but lingering long enough to be subsumed in the coat's wonderful glow, before he opens the door and disappears into the dark and stormy lane.

The next day could not come soon enough – the boy could not sleep, so excited was he at the prospect of wearing the coat again, and yet worrying, that it was all a dream, that the incredible sensations the coat had stirred in him had been simply his imagination. It was indeed easy to doubt that what had happened had been real, so impossible was it to believe that such sensations *could* have been real. But as the old tailor slipped the coat over his shoulders, he felt the same joy rise in him, the same euphoria, as the world once again transformed, from its usual drab and familiar hues to one of sparkling, golden intensity!

And yet, as before, when it came time to leave, a terrible storm appeared to be raging outside, and the boy declined the offer to take the coat away, acquiescing to the old tailor's advice, that perhaps it would be best to allow the coat to remain safe in the shop.

So the boy returned, day after day, and it never changed, the same rush of excitement filling him, as the old tailor silently helped him to discard his own coat and put on the golden one, to be instantly and ecstatically swathed in the same glorious golden transformation.

Not once did the wonder of it diminish - if anything, as the days, weeks, months passed, it seemed to become stronger, the golden aura becoming deeper, richer, brighter. It spurred the boy to spend as much time as possible at the shop – he would rush there almost in a panic, desperate to reach the shop as fast as he could, to make the most of the precious time that he could spend there, to wear the coat and delight in its astounding and surreal embrace. Every second he could do so became immeasurably valuable. He would stretch those seconds into as many minutes as feasible, and the minutes into hours. But never was it enough: it was an agonising joy, these moments, such as they were, whether a second or an hour, of such exquisite comfort and pleasure that were always over, far too soon.

Yet every day, when the tailor would ask him, his offer apparently so measured and impartial, whether he wished to take the coat away, the boy would decline. He was increasingly conscious of the storm which raged perpetually outside, its degree of tempest variable certainly, but always of such perceived force, that when the tailor suggested, as he always did, perhaps it would be best, best to let the coat remain in the shop, the boy dutifully agreed. What else could he do? He would never risk the damage that the terrible storm might inflict upon the coat. More so, something, perhaps something in the old tailor's manner of asking, something made the boy convinced that it would be an intolerable thing to do, to take the coat from the shop.

So the days steadily passed, into months, and eventually years. It was impossible at times for the boy to visit every day, his opportunities to do so inevitably constricted – sometimes it was every day, once a day, and sometimes even, more than once a day. However, at other times he couldn't come for weeks, sometimes months. Regardless, though - every time he put on the coat, the same wonderful golden sensation consumed him. It became a willing addiction. Where initially it was almost a *discomfort*, the degree of comfort that being enveloped in the coat provoked, increasingly and with greater ease the boy developed an ability to give himself up completely to it. He learnt to abandon himself, utterly and entirely – not only was the world transformed, but everything the boy thought too, his memories, his hopes, his dreams, everything, became coloured and enriched by the golden aura. It became subsequently ever more difficult to discern what was real and what was not: where before the wearing of the coat had been the fantasy, when not wearing it, the life the boy led seemed totally pointless, a fruitless existence, invalid and all the more unreal because of it. The boy never felt this more than when he was taken very ill, and was unable to visit the shop for some considerable number of months. In the enforced separation, terrible doubts assailed him, less so pertaining to the value of the world the coat created, despite the absence of it, but rather concerning the life he led without it. When he could at last resume his visits to the shop, it was such a heartening and powerful affirmation of the coat's place in the boy's life, so resolutely joyful was it to feel its immediate and unconditional caress.

Throughout, and constantly attendant, was the old tailor. He always maintained a discreet distance from the boy – they hardly spoke, other than some few words of greeting and their perennial discussion at the boy's departure. Sometimes he would sit with the boy, sometimes he would fuss unnecessarily over him, but more often than not he would busy himself in the workroom, and leave the boy alone. Sometimes, admittedly only occasionally, he became annoyed at the boy, angry even, and on such occasions the boy would leave much earlier than he intended, saddened and upset by the old tailor's abrupt manner. Usually however, the old man's mood was much more measured, of a conciliatory and dutifully patient nature.

Similarly the boy maintained his own good grace, polite, and contented to be wrapped up in the coat. Occasionally, however, he too would get angry, angry at the storm that never, ever, abated, that prevented him from taking the coat out from the confines of the shop, out and into the freedom of the city. He would stand at the door, his hand shaking upon the handle, close, so close to walking out, storm or no storm. But he never did, at the last moment retreating, back to the safety and security of the shop, slightly ashamed and bitterly confused.

At such moments he was grateful for the old tailor's persistent and reassuring presence – but often this constant presence was a source of some frustration. The old tailor was *always* there, and the boy could not help but feel inhibited, to some degree, by it. Only on a very few select and rare occasions would the old tailor go out, on some errand or other, and these occasions became for the boy, the absolute and most wondrous of moments. With the old tailor absent, in the uncommon solitude, the boy could sacrifice himself, entirely and without reservation, to the coat's delight. It would seem on these occasions that the boy dissolved completely into the coat's golden aura, that there was no distinction whatsoever between where the boy began and where the coat ended:

he would feel as if he had disappeared, he and the coat too, and both transported, formless, and transformed into a pure, golden light, that floated, endless and forever in a golden world of its own perfect creation. Such moments transcended any language, and the boy could only treasure them as, simply, the most profound of unforeseen blessings.

But on other occasions his visits to the shop could be subject to appalling consequence and circumstance. One awful day the boy arrived to find that the shop had been ravaged by a terrible fire – and to his horror, his coat, his beautiful coat, damaged, charred and burnt. The boy was inconsolable – his memory afterwards was blurred, and all he could recall was that he sat, hopeless and utterly distraught, on the blackened floor of the smoke charred shop, weeping and lost, the coat lying destroyed and smouldering over his knees.

Through the lingering and acerbic haze, the old tailor's voice drew him from his dark despair. 'I can repair it' he said.

'But how? How? It is ruined!' the boy howled, tears streaming down his blackened face.

'Trust me' the old tailor said, kindly. The boy looked up at him, doubt and hope blossoming in equal measure. The old man held out his gnarled hand.

'Come' he said. 'Let me show you……'

Leading the little boy into the workroom, the old tailor laid the coat out over the long workbench that ran down the centre of the room. He cut away all the parts that were so irrevocably and irreparably damaged, and then with hands deft beyond belief, proceeded to re-stitch the coat, slowly and patiently. His hands moved with an incomprehensible fluidity and skill, and the boy could only watch in bewildered awe, as the old tailor worked, cutting, stitching, then cleaning, and brushing with accurate and steady dexterity, until at last the coat was once again complete.

Hanging it up on the mannequin, difficult, indeed impossible as it might be to witness, the coat seemed to be finer than it had been before. But upon the wearing of it, the boy could only wonder at the truth of such a perception – indeed, the coat *was* more perfect than it had been!

'Well?' asked the old tailor.

'I can't believe it! I can't believe it. How did you do that?'

The old man only smiled, his eyes blank and distant.

'Can you teach me?' the boy insisted. 'Can you?'

'Certainly' replied the old tailor, surprising the boy with his easy accord. 'If you wish to learn' he added, soberly.

'Oh I do, I do' replied the boy enthusiastically.

From that day, and every day thereafter, the old tailor would reveal some secret of his unique and wonderful trade: measuring, cutting, stitching, sewing, brushing and grooming. He would explain which needles were appropriate for which cloth, which pins were best for the temporary holding of the chosen material. He would show the boy how different cloth might fall, and how it might lie depending on how it was cut. He introduced the boy to the almost endless selection of threads that might be employed, how to form beading, how to attach buttons, make cuffs, lapels, linings and pockets. Slowly and painstakingly the boy mastered every aspect of the craft, assisting the old tailor as he worked on the coats hanging in the workroom, and applying his newly acquired abilities to the constant maintenance of his own golden coat.

But more appalling disasters were to befall the coat; disasters that would rain such wanton destruction on the garment, the boy could only wonder whether some malign and vindictive influence was at work. On another awful occasion the coat was again damaged by fire, and then on another, the shop was burgled and the coat cut, slashed repeatedly in an apparent act of unreasonable and spiteful maliciousness, and again, on yet another occasion, the storm blew in the shop window, scarring the coat with broken glass and staining it with freezing and dirty water.

Every time, the boy repaired the coat himself, his eyes blinded by tears, but trusting to the skill that he'd forged, and that abided serenely, in his hands and fingers. And once the repairs were complete, no matter how damaged the coat might have been, it always appeared finer, stronger and more perfect than before.

Time passes once again, some considerable time. The old tailor watches over the boy, as he becomes increasingly accomplished in his own right, and suggests one day that perhaps the boy might consider making a coat himself? The boy is truly humbled that the tailor would think him capable of such, and throws himself into the task with absolute delight.

It seems obvious to him that he might try and replicate his own golden coat, and so, hanging it up on a mannequin in the workroom as a guide, the boy sets about trying to copy it. He works long into the night, every night, for weeks, the storm constantly raging overhead, rain battering incessantly on the roof-light above him. Despite however spending such a dedicated amount of time working at it, he simply cannot come anywhere close to matching his own coat. All his attempts seem feeble by comparison. It frustrates the boy terribly. Finally his frustration boils over, and in a fit of uncommon rage, he smashes the workroom, tearing up all his pathetic efforts, over-turning the workbench, and in the process knocking over the mannequin. His golden coat sprawls from it, to lie crumpled and useless on the floor.

Sitting disconsolate in the ruined workroom, surrounded by the tatters of discarded cloth and threads, his own coat left to lie where it fell, the boy finally gives up.

'I can't do this' he complains, crying, to the old tailor. 'I've tried and tried, but I just can't!'

The old tailor looks at the boy, absently picking up and then dropping some of the remnants of the cloth that lie everywhere.

'You did not listen to what I suggested.'

The boy looks back at him, confused. The old tailor ignores him, as he rights the workbench, gathers up the shreds of tattered cloth, separates them, rolls them up and lays them out tidily. He rights the mannequin, before then lifting the golden coat from the floor, and, with the usual courtesy, settles it over the boy's shoulders. Its familiar golden aura once more, envelopes the boy.

'Try again' the old tailor says, 'and try a different shade.....' he suggests, before he leaves the workroom.

The boy could not have explained how it was that he was able to create the coat he then made. Those same small hands that had led him into the shop, so long ago, seemed now to guide him, effortlessly, as he selected cloth, measured, cut, sewed and stitched, over and over, working as if, once again, in a trance. He completely lost track of time – he would sleep all day, collapsed across the workbench, and immediately upon waking, he would begin his work, working ceaselessly through the night, until, with the coming of the dawn, he would then once again fall asleep, his head on his arms, exhausted. Overhead the storm continued to rage, but the boy no longer heard it, nor did he hear the rain that continued to pound upon the glass. Lightning would flash across the workbench, appearing almost to select which pieces of cloth to use, and on occasion when the storm abated, the moonlight streamed across the material chosen, to soak into it, colouring it, and leaving it to glow, deep and warm with a ghostly light. The stars too would seem drop from their distant place, to pepper the coat with sparkling embellishments, and in the candlelit gloom of the workroom the coat began to take shape, bit by bit pieced together upon the mannequin.

Eventually, with every piece of cloth and every piece of thread used, the coat was complete. The boy sat back, at last, and, despite his intense weariness, despite too the pain in fingers that ached and were bloodied from the endless nights of sewing, he delighted and justifiably took pride in his achievement: a coat, a gorgeous, and incredible, coat, every part of it, of resplendent and shimmering silver.

And as he drifted into a satisfied slumber, he was aware of the old tailor, hovering over him.

'I can't do any more' whispered the boy. The tailor's gnarled hands gently stroked his hair, his words reaching the boy as if through a fog: 'You have done enough' he said, as the boy slipped into unconsciousness. 'It is beautiful…'

When the boy next awoke, he was immediately aware of a strange and unfamiliar silence. Rubbing his eyes, and lifting his head from the workbench, the first thing he noticed was the mannequin: it was bare! His silver coat was gone!

A note was pinned in its place. In a shaky but sophisticated script, it read:

'To my dear companion,

You have created a coat as fine as any I might make. As you have learnt everything that I could ever teach you, I am free now to leave, and I must therefore do so.

You have my eternal gratitude, by earning for me, my freedom. I entrust to you, in return, all my worldly goods: this shop, and everything in it. It is all I have and all I have ever known.

Even so, it is feeble recompense, for it is of meagre value, and offers you only the promise of a chance. I hope it is enough. I hope you find in it what I have found. I hope you stay, and I hope that you do not have to wait as I have.

Please, if you can forgive me for the time already I have asked of you, take it.'

Lying on the workbench were the old tailor's glasses, his fingerless gloves, and his measuring tape. The boy stared at them, the unsigned note hanging limp in his hand. He couldn't quite grasp what he was seeing, what it was that the note was telling him. Then the truth of it dawned on him, as he stood there in the silence: the tailor was gone! And, in the same instant, the boy thought: 'He has left me! He's left me and he has taken my coat, my silver coat!'

In a panic, he rushed from the workroom, but was immediately pulled up short. For there, hanging in the window, was the silver coat. It was not to the coat, however, that the boys' attention was drawn. For, through the window, staring intently and unblinking at it, was a little girl.

The boy stopped, motionless, and hiding in the shadow of the shop, watched the little girl in return. She didn't move, did not take her gaze from the coat, her face rapt and frozen, bright and glittering, sea-blue eyes wide and fixed upon it. Not a hair on her head, hair so blonde as to appear almost white, moved, neither did her round pretty face, her tiny hands, nothing. Everything about her was transfixed, caught as if in some crippling and hypnotic trance, rendering her as immobile as a miniature statue. Something, some sound perhaps, suddenly disturbed her – she turned with a frightened look, and dashed in an instant away, disappearing into the darkness of the winding lane.

The boy remained standing in the shadows for some considerable time, softly haunted by the image of the little girl's face, of her rigid and yet amazed expression, provoking distant memories from his own childhood. Had he too stared with such an expression, at his golden coat? It was so long ago. So, so long ago. He looked down at his coat, all of a sudden noticing how worn it had become, worn and shabby. He'd neglected it, all the time he'd spent making the silver coat, and not once had he thought to maintain his own. The cuffs were frayed, as was the collar, it was marked here and there by tailor's chalk, and the material everywhere creased and wrinkled. There were even little tears in the fabric, and a button or two missing. Somehow it seemed to drain him, such sad observations, and he settled wearily, dazed and confused, into one of the two seats beside the fire. Long forgotten thoughts overwhelmed him, drowning him in memories from long, long ago, of standing, for hours and hours, bathed in a rich and glorious light. He was drawn by such memories into a strange yet warm slumber, as if in a melted dream, before he finally fell into a deep, deep sleep.

He had no idea how long he slept, but when he awoke, she was there again, the little girl, staring as intently as she had before. The boy stared back, unable to take his eyes off her. She was small, too small for the silver coat. It would never fit her as it was. He would need to make some adjustments ......

And so it was, that every day from then on, the boy began to alter the silver coat, his keen eye noting the slightest of changes in the little girl's physique, even the tiniest of things, and in turn he would adjust the coat to suit. There was hardly a day went by that the little girl did not appear at the window, and the boy would watch her, watch her intently for as long as she might stay, standing hidden from her by the darkness of the shop's interior. And every day, after she departed, the storm would reappear, raining perhaps less than it had before, but still of such severity to cause the wind to howl deep and low, scattering dust and papers everywhere through the lane: and he would retire to the workroom, make some small change here, some minor alteration there.

At first the adjustments were to accommodate obvious discrepancies, her height, her girth, or the length of her limbs, but as time went on, the adjustments were made to accommodate things, things less obvious – how she held herself, simply standing, her various postures, or how she walked, her gait, the pace of her steps, or how she smiled, albeit this only happened occasionally, but to accommodate how her face might change as she did so; or how she frowned; how her hair fell across her shoulders, how every strand might lie; how her hands might curl or uncurl as some thought might worry her; even how she breathed, how her small frame rose and fell, in tandem with her moods, whether she might appear slightly happier, or sadder for some unknown reason. The most subtle of changes, the boy noticed, every little thing, everything that the little girl was, the boy missed nothing – and every observation provoked some change in the silver coat. Every single one.

As time passed, the little girl grew and grew, and as she did so, the boy aged with her – his hands became gnarled, arthritic, and he took to wearing the old tailor's fingerless gloves for protection and warmth. His eyes too became dim, dimmer and dimmer, until eventually he needed to wear the old tailor's delicate glasses to be able to see, to make the perpetual changes to the silver coat. He became, slowly but steadily, old, an old, old man, bent and wrinkled, as he spent endless hours sitting in the workroom, patiently and carefully adjusting the coat.

And with every stitch that he put to the silver coat, with every touch, it seemed that his own golden coat, slowly but steadily, also was repaired.

Inevitably, more time passes, much more time, and then one day the shop bell gently tinkles, and there, standing in the shop window, is the little girl. The old man watches her from the workroom: she is not so little any more, he thinks to himself. Not a girl at all, but a woman for sure, a beautiful young woman. Was *I* ever so young, he wonders? And if I was, was I ever as graceful and elegant as she? He cannot recall, and even if he could, he certainly could not be accused of retaining any remnant of such youthful vigour any longer. Feeling terribly the years of his age, he shuffles out into the shop front, an old, old man.

The young woman has her back to him, with her hand reaching out, her fingers uncurling ever, ever so slowly towards the silver coat. She does not hear the old man approach.

'Can I help you, miss?' he asks.

The woman turns with a start, her eyes still of such a sparkling bright sea-blue, her lovely face framed by hair of such a luxurious and luminous pale yellow, still so pale as to appear almost white.

'This coat?' she says, nervously but with an affected casualness, indicating to the coat in the window.

'The silver coat?' the old man asks.

'Yes' she says. 'How much is it?'

'Oh, I'm afraid that coat is not for sale' says the old man.

He sees in her face the same distress, the same appalling sense of loss that he too had once felt. His want, however, is not to confound her, as he had been.

'But...perhaps, you might wish to try it on?' he offers, as immediately and kindly as he can.

'Oh yes....but, no. No. I don't know.'

'Please – it may be that this coat is not for sale, but that does not mean it has no owner.'

The young woman looks at him, confused, a slight frown creasing the otherwise absolute smoothness of her pale yet ever so slightly pink complexion.

'Please' the old man repeats, smiling, and still as kindly as he is able, 'please, I would be most grateful if you would try it on - you would be doing me a tremendous favour. It has never been worn, you see, this coat, in fact no-one has ever even asked to do so, before now.'

With a rather sad and delicate sincerity, the woman replies: 'I would, really, I would love to…but…if it's not for sale, really, I couldn't.'

The old man looks at her, steadily for a moment, with his blank, watery eyes. Her eyes, so innocent and so fragile, yet with a resolve in them too, look back as steadily into his.

'I tell you what,' he says, 'if you would be prepared to agree, perhaps we might make a deal?'

'A deal?'

'Yes, a deal. If you would be prepared to try this coat on, and if you find then that it does indeed fit, the deal is: it is yours, you may have it.'

'I may have it?'

'Yes. Yes, you may.'

The young woman pauses for a second. 'And what if it doesn't?' she asks, unable to conceal an element of awkward suspicion in her voice.

'Well, then, you have lost nothing' replies the old man, frankly, 'but if it does, then, I promise, you may have it. You may think of it as your coat.'

'I have always thought it so…..' the woman says wistfully.

'Well then, please, let me….?'

Without allowing her any further deliberation, the old man helps the woman out of her own coat. He then lifts the silver coat gently from the mannequin and holds it open for her. She hesitates only for a second, before slipping her arms into the sleeves, and as the old man helps settle the coat onto the young woman's shoulders, he cannot fail to notice the expression of absolute joy that shivers fleetingly over her.

'Well?' he asks.

'It's......perfect' she says, softly.

'It fits?'

'Oh yes, yes.....yes, it fits. I could never have imagined how... how perfectly!'

'Well, yes. Yes, of course. And why would it not?' says the old man, gently still smoothing down the coat over the young woman's shoulders.

She looks at him, confused once again.

'I don't understand' she says. 'You make it sound like it, I don't know – ......'

'What?' the old man prompts, as the woman leaves hanging, her thought, unfinished.

'I don't know. Like it was made ......just for me?'

The old man smiles his kindly smile. 'Well, if it feels so, then perhaps it must be so. Perhaps ......only you can really know, only you can really say, whether or not it is your coat.'

The young woman cannot help but stare into the persistent gaze of the old man. She runs her hands slowly down over her arms. Tears suddenly appear in her eyes.

'I-' she begins.

The old man interrupts her.

'Take it' he says, quietly.

'No, really, really, I couldn't.'

'Take it. Please. Take it. It is your coat.'

The young woman continues to stare at the old man, he staring insistently back at her. He sees her lips quiver ever so slightly, before she turns her face away, to look intently out through the shop window.

'But I must pay you something for it. Please.' she says, all of a sudden responsibly pragmatic.

'No, really, really there is no need' the old man answers her. 'I have earned enough, more than enough, in the making of it. If I had to put that into monetary terms, and apply it to the sale of this garment, its price would be...... priceless. And who then could afford to purchase such a garment? Well obviously, no-one. It would remain therefore abandoned, here on this sorry mannequin. And no coat is made to be left so. Particularly, if I may be so bold, a coat as fine as this.'

'Oh yes, it is, it is fine, indeed...it is......beautiful.'

'Well then, you would be doing me a great honour if you were to accept it. Please take it. You may never get another coat like it. And of course, if you ever feel the need, you can always return it.'

'Oh, no, I don't think I'd ever-' the young woman says, involuntarily and almost shocked at the old tailor's suggestion. He smiles at her again, forgivingly.

'No, no, I suspect not' he says, patting her gently on the arm.

Still however, the young woman does not move, and they stand, side by side, saying nothing, staring silently out through the shop window. The sun begins to set, and the light inside the shop slowly too begins to fade. As the sun's rays finally disappear from view, down behind the dark silhouette of the city in the distance, the young woman, with her arms wrapped around herself, says in a voice barely more than a whisper: 'I don't know what to do. I don't know.'

The old man looks at her, but says nothing. He leaves her standing in the window for a while, to fuss quietly about, tidying up the shop. There is however, very little for him to put away – there are no shirts left, no ties, socks, or braces. He closes all the empty slender, polished drawers, and locks the glass topped counter, empty too of cufflinks and tie pins. In the workroom, the countless rolls of fabrics and cloth are all gone, and the mannequins also, stand, mute, naked and unadorned. The old man lines them up, and then lays his tools neatly on the workbench, beside his measuring tape, finger-less gloves and glasses. Lastly he cleans out the grate in the small fireplace, before re-joining the woman, to stand again beside her, silently staring through the shop window.

They stand for a long, long while, so long that time almost seems to stop. Ever so gradually the colours in the sky change, to shades of such intense purples, ambers and reds.

'Isn't it a beautiful evening?' says the old man, eventually.

'Yes' the woman replies, again, so softly, 'yes it is…'

'Hard to believe that something could be so beautiful, is it not? Hard to believe that something so beautiful could even be real, don't you think?'

'Yes' the woman agrees, softly still.

The old man puts his hand gently on the woman's arm. 'And it's hard, perhaps the hardest thing of all, to believe that such beauty could have been made, perhaps, made for you, and just for you? Hard, is it not, to believe you could be deserving of such beauty? A beauty, more perfect than you could ever imagine?'

The woman pauses, before answering in a voice, defeated and frail but somehow with a strength imbued by the admission: 'Yes'.

If the woman had looked, she would have seen the old man smile, and his eyes, become luminous and blank, but with a glow too of such intimate warmth and tender generosity.

'And yet, once seen, once felt, such beauty, so undeniably real and perfect, is it not easier to accept than it is to deny, the simple and profound truth of it: that this beauty *is* yours? It is yours, and no one else's, and it always has been, and always, always, will be?'

The woman says nothing, nothing for some considerable time, before the old man hears her say, in a voice still so, so soft and deathly quiet: 'Yes', and then, again, 'yes', louder and as if only to herself.

Suddenly she turns to the old man, unashamedly smiling, tears glittering in her eyes. 'Thank you' she says, her words filled with a resounding and untamed joy: 'Thank you, thank you for my coat!' She kisses him lightly on the cheek, before turning, just as abruptly, and steps lightly out of the shop.

The old man stands for another long, long while, looking out through the shop window at the sunset. He waits and waits, expecting the storm to come. But it doesn't. Instead the colours in the sky become completely fixed, unchanging, to cast a warm and curious light upon everything, as the old man looks around, colours everything that he sees. Everything,

everything has a sparkling and iridescent golden aura about it. Everything.

He takes one last look around, and then the old man too steps from the empty shop, to walk outside for the first time, in his beautiful golden coat.

Epilogue:
In the humid, summer evening, little boys still career irreverently through the streets of the vast and great, dark city – they don't notice an old man limping, hunched and tired, slowly along the pavement, huddled in an old coat. The little boys don't see him, in fact, no one does.

If any had taken the time, and looked closer, they might have noticed that the old man's attire was not nearly as shabby as it might first appear – the coat wrapped around him was not ragged at all, but it was in fact a rather fine thing, worn certainly, but well crafted, well made, well fitted and truly, elegant. And if they had looked further, they might have noticed that the old man himself, despite his age, was also not as worn out as he might at first seem – he had a curious glint in his watery eyes, and a gentle smile on his dry lips.

They might see these things, and they might wonder at the curiousness of it, of the old man's attire, his strange, contented demeanour, outwardly at odds with the overall impression of a man, so aged and redundant. It would forever perplex, however slightly – this old man, so indifferent to the distractions of the life all around him, caretaker of a secret they could not fathom.

But then those witnesses, no matter how much time they might look, would never be able to see what the old man could see, reflected in every shop window that he passes. They would see just the same old man, broken and alone – but this old man, he sees something else entirely. He sees reflected, a man, a youthful man, walking proudly and erect, resplendent in a glorious golden coat, strong, fearless, striding gracefully and confidently, without pain or regret, secure in the knowledge that with his beautiful coat wrapped around him, he would live happily ever after.

THE UNHAPPY 'ONE'

Once there was a tiny number,
A sad and lonely little one.
It was the least of all of them -
And being so was no fun!

Although they didn't mean to,
It made her feel so small,
How much the other numbers had,
When she had nought at all.

She'd listen to their perfect claims
Although it caused her grief,
To hear them talk about her
In refrain, without relief:

Chorus:
Well at least on this we can agree
All are bigger than some.
And even if that's not enough,
Well at least we're bigger than one!

10

The ten did forever boast
'I am better than the rest,
Coz' I'm the biggest of all of you -
And biggest is simply the best!'

9

Nine would just shake her head
Clearly unimpressed.
'Size is not what counts' she'd say
'It's curves that count, no contest!'

8

'Curves?' would query the number eight,
'Well in that I do excel.
Mine are perfect, you must concede
And two, not just one, circle!'

Chorus:
Well at least on this we can agree
All are bigger than some.
And even if that's not enough,
Well at least we're bigger than one!

7

'You might be all above me'
Said sharply number seven,
'But I go higher than all of you
Straight t(w)o seventh heaven!'

6

'Heavens above? Don't make me sick!'
Sneered the six by six by six
'Down below's where seven sins
In a helluva' place, 'ol Nick's!'

5

'Hell and heaven: but add or subtract'
Contented five dismissed.
'But I with ease do multiply!'
['And like a letter too' S hissed.]

Chorus:
Well at least on this we can agree
All are bigger than some.
And even if that's not enough,
Well at least we're bigger than one!

4
'I may just be, one half of eight
But too I'm two all square,
And the *worlds'* within *my* corners'
Four securely did declare.

3
'I may just *look,* like half an eight'
Primed three with much ado.
'But only I can make a crowd,
Which is more than two can do!'

2
'Too true too', agreed the two
'But two's company too is fun
And even if it isn't true,
I'm still twice as big as one!'

Chorus:
Well at least on this we can agree
All are bigger than some.
And even if that's not enough,
Well at least we're bigger than one!

0

The zero looked, up at the one
And noted her sad demeanour.
How could the others treat her so?
How could they be so meaner?

So the zero tried to cheer her up
'Never you mind', it said.
'You are better than all of them.'
But the one just shook her head.

'It's true' the nought insisted
'If they could only see,
That without you they are nothing.
They're made from you, you see?'

The number one remained depressed
And *still* she hung her head,
So the zero tried to make it plain,
And repeated what it said:

'You think that *you* are nothing
Well zero tells you true
That nothing comes from nothing,
And that couldn't be said of you.'

'Without you *they* are nothing
Nothing, just like me.
They may never know this,
But only *you* can make them be.'

From that day on, the number one
Never felt so sad
For if she ever felt that way
She thought on what nought said:

(New) Chorus:
'So when the others state their claims
That render you undone
Remember, that they are only words
When you're a number, number **1** *!'*

Afterword

"One does not become enlightened by imagining figures of light, but by making the darkness conscious."

C.G.Jung

Thanks Martin, for the quote – you'll know this I'm sure, but it occurred to me that even angels may doubt......

MA

Printed in Great Britain
by Amazon